"If there's anything I can do, just ask. I could help with the search."

Ryker shook his head. "We can't risk civilians running around those old mines. Though if we narrow the search area, we might call on search and rescue."

"If that happens, I'll be there." Harper looked down at her desk, suddenly feeling awkward. "And if you ever just want to talk, I'm here for that, too."

"Thanks." He covered her hand with his, and she felt the shock of that contact and looked into his eyes.

She saw the same awareness there—a connection she had thought long severed flickering to life.

COLORADO KIDNAPPING

CINDI MYERS

INTRIGUE

Harlequin® INTRIGUE™

Recycling programs for this product may not exist in your area.

ISBN-13: 978-1-335-45691-5

Colorado Kidnapping

Copyright © 2024 by Cynthia Myers

For questions and comments about the quality of this book, please contact us at CustomerService@Harlequin.com.

TM and ® are trademarks of Harlequin Enterprises ULC.

Harlequin Enterprises ULC
22 Adelaide St. West, 41st Floor
Toronto, Ontario M5H 4E3, Canada
www.Harlequin.com

Printed in Lithuania

MIX
Paper | Supporting responsible forestry
FSC® C021394

Cindi Myers is the author of more than seventy-five novels. When she's not plotting new romance storylines, she enjoys skiing, gardening, cooking, crafting and daydreaming. A lover of small-town life, she lives with her husband and two spoiled dogs in the Colorado mountains.

Books by Cindi Myers

Harlequin Intrigue

Eagle Mountain: Criminal History

Mile High Mystery
Colorado Kidnapping

Eagle Mountain: Critical Response

Deception at Dixon Pass
Pursuit at Panther Point
Killer on Kestrel Trail
Secrets of Silverpeak Mine

Eagle Mountain Search and Rescue

Eagle Mountain Cliffhanger
Canyon Kidnapping
Mountain Terror
Close Call in Colorado

Visit the Author Profile page at Harlequin.com.

CAST OF CHARACTERS

Ryker Vernon—Rayford County's newest sheriff's deputy has returned to his hometown as a single dad to raise his daughter and make a fresh start. But the past won't leave him alone.

Charlotte Vernon—The happy four-year-old has weathered the storms of her parents' divorce well and is the focus of Ryker's energy.

Harper Stanick—Ryker's high school sweetheart secretly mourns the loss of her first love, but she's not sure the unhappiness of their past relationship bodes well for the future.

Kim Vernon Davis—Ryker married Kim because she was pregnant, but she proved unfaithful and unwilling to stay to be a mother to Charlotte.

Micky Davis—Kim's second husband is an ex-con and drifter whom Ryker wants to keep far away from the ones he loves.

Chapter One

The little girl squealed with delight as she ran across the playground, blond hair flying out behind her. When she stumbled and fell she popped up immediately, still laughing, and resumed her race with her companions. Sheriff's deputy Ryker Vernon, standing just on the other side of the playground fence, swallowed past the catch in his throat and marveled at his daughter's—Charlotte's—sunny disposition. Where did she get that from? Not from her mother. Kim had a decidedly darker outlook on life, one that had led her to eventually leave him and her daughter behind.

Charlotte didn't get her happy personality from Ryker, either. Five years as a law enforcement officer had shown him too much of the bad side of people to make him inclined toward lightheartedness. Yet here was Charlotte, bubbly personality intact despite her mother's desertion and their recent relocation back to his hometown of Eagle Mountain, Colorado.

Charlotte reached the apple tree that apparently marked the finish line of the race and stopped, puffing for breath, her round cheeks bright pink, deep dimples on either side of her smiling lips. She turned and caught sight of Ryker and all but jumped for joy. "Daddy!" she shouted, and took off toward him.

Her teacher, Sheila Lindstrom, caught up with her just as Charlotte raced past the boundary of the fence and, also spotting Ryker, accompanied the child to meet him. He was glad to see the teacher was so diligent. "Hello, Deputy Vernon," Sheila said as Charlotte threw her arms around Ryker's legs. "I didn't know you were picking up Charlotte this afternoon." She tucked a strand of hair a shade paler than Charlotte's behind one ear and smiled up at him in a way that reminded him he was a single man in a small town where the dating pool might be thought of as limited.

He didn't return the smile, and took a step back, hoping to give the impression that he wasn't interested. Not that Sheila wasn't a perfectly nice woman, but he was juggling enough right now, with a new job, a new home and a little girl to raise. He didn't need the complications that came with a relationship. "Charlotte's grandmother will be picking her up, as usual," he said. "I just started my shift and since Charlotte will be in bed by the time I'm back home, I swung by to say hello." He rested his hand on the little girl's head as she beamed up at him.

"That's so sweet," Sheila said, and tilted her head to one side, blue eyes still fixed on him as if he was some delectable treat.

"Ryker! What are you doing here? Is everything all right?"

He and Sheila and Charlotte all turned to see Ryker's mother, Wanda Vernon, hurrying up the sidewalk toward them. Slender and athletic, with dark curls past her shoulders, Wanda Vernon looked younger than her fifty years, but right now worry lines creased her normally smooth forehead.

"Nothing's wrong, Mom," Ryker reassured her. "I just stopped by to say hello to Charlotte."

"Grammie, I found a horny toad at recess this morning, but teacher made me put it back," Charlotte announced.

"You know our wild friends are happier remaining in the wild," Sheila said.

"I know," Charlotte said. "But he was so pretty. He had gold eyes and a gold and brown body with bumps on it. Amy thought he was icky, but I thought he was beautiful."

Ryker hid his smile behind his hand. That was his daughter. She had never met an insect or amphibian or item from nature that frightened or repelled her.

"Horned toads are very interesting," Wanda said. "But it's always best to just look at them, and not touch. You wouldn't want to accidentally hurt one."

"Oh, I would never do that!" Charlotte looked offended at the idea.

Ryker's shoulder-mounted radio crackled, and the dispatcher's voice came through clearly. "Unit five, report to Dixon Pass, mile marker 97, to assist at accident site. EMS and SAR on the way."

Ryker keyed the mike, aware that everyone within earshot had turned to stare. "Unit five responding. I'm on my way." He squatted down until he was eye level with his daughter. "I have to go now, honey," he said. "Can I have a kiss goodbye?"

She responded by throwing her arms around him and kissing his cheek. "Be careful, Daddy," she said.

"I always am, sweetheart. You be a good girl for Grammie and Grandpa."

"I always am!" she echoed.

"Be careful," his mother and Sheila said in unison as he nodded goodbye, then jogged toward his sheriff's department SUV.

He turned the vehicle toward the highway and switched

on lights and sirens to cut a clear path toward the accident. As he passed the preschool he caught a glimpse of Charlotte with his mother on the sidewalk. The little girl was smiling and waving. Some of the heaviness in his heart lifted, as it always did when he was with her. Through all the upheaval in her young life, Charlotte was resilient.

Ryker was trying to follow her example, to roll with the punches life threw at him, or at least do a better job of hiding his bruises.

"It looks like the vehicle rolled several times before it came to land on that ledge." Eagle Mountain Search and Rescue Captain Danny Irwin stood with the cluster of volunteers on the side of the highway as they peered over the side at the battered silver sedan wedged between a boulder and the cliff approximately one hundred yards below. "You can see pieces of the car that broke off every time the car bounced."

Harper Stanick, a search and rescue rookie, winced as she took in the trail of debris and the battered vehicle. It looked like this was going to be her first body recovery. She had been warned this was part of search and rescue and told herself she was prepared, but still. What would a person look like after enduring that kind of trauma?

"I saw movement!" Paramedic Hannah Richards, who had arrived with the ambulance but joined her fellow SAR volunteers in surveying the scene, pointed at the vehicle. "There's someone alive in there!"

Her exclamation prodded them into action. Danny directed volunteers Eldon Ramsey and Tony Meissner to rig ropes for a rappel onto the ledge beside the car. Harper joined fellow trainees Grace Wilcox, Anna Trent and veteran Christine Mercer in gathering helmets, harnesses, a litter and other gear they would need to stabilize the injured survivor and get them to safety above. Danny radioed to have a medical helicopter land two miles away at the soccer fields in town to meet the ambulance and transport the injured person or persons to the hospital in Junction.

"What can I do to help?"

At the sound of the man's voice, deep and slightly hoarse, Harper fumbled the safety helmets she had been charged with, and had to juggle to keep from losing one. "Careful," Christine said.

"Close the highway, if you haven't already," Danny said. "Clear space on the side of the highway for us to go down and keep everyone back from the edge. We don't want anyone else falling in, or kicking rocks down on top of us as we work."

Harper turned to see who Danny was talking to and this time she did drop the helmets. Seven years since she had laid eyes on Ryker Vernon and she might have thought she was hallucinating him now, except that it made perfect sense for him to be here. Ryker was from Eagle Mountain, just like her. The first thing she had done when she moved back was to snoop around, long enough to determine he had left town, but apparently he had returned. Just like her.

What didn't make sense was that Ryker was now apparently a cop. No mistaking that khaki uniform or the gun on his hip. Ryker, a cop? The motorcycle-riding bad boy who had practically sent her mother into a faint the first time he showed up at their house to pick Harper up for a date was a law enforcement officer?

And damned if he didn't look just as good in that uniform as he had in his motorcycle leathers all those years ago. Better even, his chest a little broader, his jaw firmer. The Ryker she had known had been barely eighteen, still with a bit of the boy about him. This version of him was harder. A man.

"Hey, earth to Harper. Are you okay?" Christine followed Harper's gaze toward the officer who stood with Danny and she grinned. "I take it this is your first encounter with the newest addition to the sheriff's department," she said. "He's pretty easy on the eyes, isn't he?" She nudged Harper with her elbow. "I hear he's a single dad. Maybe when we're done here you can introduce yourself."

The bottom dropped out of Harper's stomach at the word *dad*. Ryker was a father? When? Who?

"Pull your eyes back in your head and focus on the job," Christine said, her voice firm. "You can chase after the cop later."

Harper turned her back on Ryker. "I'm not going to chase after him," she said. "I was just surprised. He reminds me of someone I used to know."

"Must have been a pretty special someone," Christine said. "The way you were staring at him. Like one of those cartoons, where the air fills with hearts."

"Not like that at all," Harper said, and gathered up the helmets she had dropped. Maybe at one time she was that gaga about Ryker Vernon, but those days were long past.

DESPITE HOW FAR the vehicle had rolled and the shape the car was in, three people emerged alive. Ryker watched from a distance as search and rescue volunteers descended on ropes to the ledge and worked to stabilize the vehicle, then cut most of the rest of the car away to reach the passengers trapped inside.

First up was an infant, a living testament to the effectiveness of child safety seats, as he sustained nothing more than a minor cut on his forehead from broken glass. Volunteer Eldon Ramsey carried the baby, still secured in his seat, up to the road, where the paramedics pronounced him perfectly okay then reluctantly turned him over to the Victim Services volunteer, who was tasked with locating a relative or temporary foster parent to care for him until his parents were released from the hospital.

Said parents also both survived, with several broken bones between them. They were brought up one at a time strapped into litters. The technical aspects of the maneuvers required to bring them to safety fascinated Ryker, who would admit to being nervous about heights.

"That was amazing," he said to SAR Captain Danny Irwin after the injured had been transported to the waiting helicopter and the road had been reopened. Accident investigators from Colorado State Patrol had arrived on the scene and were taking photographs and measuring skid marks for their reports, so Ryker had turned to helping the search and rescue volunteers with their gear.

"We're always looking for more volunteers," Danny said. "Deputy Jake Gwynn is on the team."

"Yeah, I hear he loves it," Ryker said. "Unfortunately, I can't commit that much time. I need to be with my daughter when I have time off."

"How old is she?" Danny asked.

"Four. It's just the two of us. And my parents. They're a big help."

Danny nodded. "My fiancée has two kids. They're a little older but I get what you mean about wanting to be there for them. They won't be little forever."

"Hey there! I heard you were back in town." Ryker turned to find Hannah Richards grinning up at him. The two of them had been in the same grade at Eagle Mountain High School way back when.

"Hi, Hannah. It's good to see you. I've only been back a couple of weeks. I'm still getting settled."

"Jake told me you signed on with the sheriff's department," she said. She held up one hand to reveal a modest diamond. "He's my fiancé, in case you haven't heard."

"He's mentioned the amazing woman he's engaged to, but I had no idea that was you."

She punched his shoulder and he pretended to recoil in pain, both of them laughing. "Hey, there's someone else here you need to see," Hannah said. She turned and waved. "Harper. Come over and see who the cat dragged in."

The name itself was enough to set Ryker's heart hammering, but seeing the woman herself made his world tilt for a moment. If anything, she was more beautiful than he remembered—her curly brown hair escaping from a twist at the back of her head, her green-hazel eyes fringed with dark lashes. Kim, to whom Ryker had confided the whole story of his and Harper's ill-fated romance, had prickled at what she interpreted as his too-fond descriptions of his teenage girlfriend. "No one is that perfect," she had protested.

But to him, Harper had been perfect. And she had reminded him of how imperfect he was. "Hello, Harper," he said, surprised at how calm and even his voice sounded. "It's good to see you again."

"Hello, Ryker. I heard you'd left town."

He had heard the same about her. "I just moved back," he said.

She was looking at him, but at the uniform, not into his eyes. "I can't believe you're a sheriff's deputy."

"Neither can I, some days." He was trying to make a joke, but the words came off flat. Hannah was watching them, her face full of questions. Did she remember that he and Harper had dated in high school?

Maybe she hadn't known. Harper's rich parents had pitched such a fit about their adored daughter seeing a guy whose father worked at the town's sewage treatment plant that he and Harper had to sneak around in order to see each other.

He had a hundred questions he wanted to ask her: What was she doing back in Eagle Mountain? What kind of work did she do? How had she ended up volunteering with search and rescue?

Was she okay? Could she ever forgive him?

"I have to go," Harper said, and turned away.

"See you around, Ryker," Hannah said. "Jake and I will have you over for dinner sometime."

"Yeah, that would be great," Ryker said, with less enthusiasm than he probably should have. He stared after Harper. She was still beautiful, all shiny hair and soft curves, but more defined now, the blurred edges of youth replaced by the firm lines of maturity. Not that she was old, but she had been through a lot in the past few years.

She had been through a lot, and he hadn't been there with her. One more failure he was having a hard time getting past.

Chapter Two

"I just found out Ryker Vernon is back in town."

Harper was still nursing her first cup of coffee the next morning when her mother called to share the news. Harper frowned, even though her mother couldn't see her. Someone had told her people could tell when you were smiling into the phone, so maybe Valerie Stanick would sense that Harper wasn't pleased about starting her day with this conversation. "Yes, I knew Ryker is in town." She took a sip of coffee. "He's a sheriff's deputy."

Valerie sniffed. "They must be desperate for officers to hire him."

"Mom!"

"Don't *mom* me. After what happened with that little boy, I'm surprised Ryker would show his face around here."

Harper's stomach knotted at the memory. "Mom! Ryker had nothing to do with Aiden Phillips's disappearance and you know it. He was completely cleared of all wrongdoing."

"But Ryker was babysitting the boy when he went missing. And they never found who killed him."

"It wasn't Ryker." Her fresh anger over this old hurt surprised Harper—anger on Ryker's behalf, but also anger that her mother was still holding that old tragedy against him. Aiden, Ryker's six-year-old cousin, had been taken from his bedroom while Ryker watched TV in the next room. "I don't need you to lecture me about Ryker Vernon. If that's why you called, I'm going to hang up now."

"I only called to warn you. I didn't want you to be upset if you ran into him accidentally."

Too late, Harper thought. "I need to go, Mom. I'm going to be late for work." She had half an hour before she had to report for work at Taylor Geographic, a company that produced detailed maps of all kinds.

"I wanted to know if you've made another date with Stan Carmichael," Valerie said. "His mother told me that he told her the two of you had a terrific time the other night."

That makes one of us, Harper thought, though she was smart enough not to say the words out loud. Barbie Carmichael was president of the Woman's Club and she and Valerie had been trying to match Harper and Stan since high school. Dinner the other night was the third time in those years that Harper had allowed herself to be pressured into going out with Stan, and the results were no better than the previous two evenings. Stan was sweet and earnest and painfully besotted with her. She had felt like a bug under a microscope throughout the entire date. Not only did he stare at her and hang on her every word, but when he touched her, his hands were always clammy. She didn't hate him, but she wasn't the least bit attracted to him. "Stan is not the man for me, Mom," she said.

"He's not a macho jerk who's going to treat you badly like Frank or Ryker." Valerie's voice rose with indignation. "I don't understand why you wouldn't want to be with a *nice* man. And Stan is a doctor! He makes a very good living."

Stan was a proctologist. She didn't want to think about how he made his living. "*Franco* did not treat me badly," she said. If anything, she had been the one to blame for their brief, failed marriage. "I never should have married him, but that was my fault. And Ryker never mistreated me, either." Not really. He had been as much a victim of circumstances as she had.

"All I can say is you didn't get this self-destructive tendency from me," Valerie said. "One of these days you're going to wake up and realize I was right."

"I really do have to go now, Mom. Talk to you soon." She ended the call, then stared into her now-cold coffee and thought about Ryker. Why had she been so unfriendly to him yesterday? He probably thought she hated him, and that wasn't it at all. As often as she had thought about what it would be like to see him again, she hadn't counted on that heart-pounding, bone-melting sense of equal parts longing and panic that had swamped her.

There was simply too much history between them. Mistakes that could never be undone.

She glanced at the clock and a different kind of panic jolted her out of her chair. She had to leave now or she would be late. Considering how few jobs in this town allowed her to employ her graphic arts degree, she didn't want to screw up and lose this one. Not when she had only been hired two months ago.

Thank goodness for work, she thought an hour later as she focused on a new trail map for a ski resort on the other side of the state. She could lose herself in a project like this and think of nothing else for the next few hours. By the time everyone else starting filing out of the office at five, her neck and back ached and her fingers were cramped around her computer mouse, but she had completed a rough outline of the map that she was proud of. She would spend the rest of the week refining the details before turning it over to another artist on staff for the colorwork.

She was gathering her belongings when her phone pinged with a text from Hannah, in the group chat they were part of with Christine and Grace. She had known Hannah since high school, but the others she was just getting to know through search and rescue. Meet us at Mo's? Hannah had typed.

Harper smiled and hit the button to reply. On my way.

Mo's Pub was packed with the usual mix of after-work locals and tourists looking for a drink or a quick meal. Harper spotted Hannah and the others at a booth near the back and pushed her way through the crowd to join them. "It looks busier than usual tonight," Harper said as she scooted into the booth next to Grace.

"It's five-dollar burger night," Christine said. "That and two-dollar draft beer pulls in a crowd."

"If there's a rescue call, we can leave from here," Grace said. "Half the team is here." She waved across the room to where Ryan Welch, Caleb Garrison and Eldon Ramsey sat side by side at the bar.

"Where's Jake tonight?" Harper asked as she helped herself from the pitcher of beer on the table. Hannah's fiancé was a SAR volunteer, too.

"He's on duty," Hannah said.

"Him and Declan." Grace made a sad face.

"Declan Owen is with the sheriff's department, too," Hannah explained in answer to Harper's confused look.

"Are there a lot of SAR volunteers dating law enforcement?" Harper asked.

"Sheri's husband is with the Colorado Bureau of Investigation," Hannah said. "And Anne is seeing Lucas Malone, with the Mesa County Sheriff's Department." She laughed. "Don't look so horrified. We work with law enforcement at a lot of accident scenes. And if anyone is going to understand the need to drop everything and rush out to an emergency, it's another first responder."

Harper nodded. Did this mean she was going to have to get used to seeing Ryker more than she had planned? Eagle Mountain was a small town, but she had really hoped to avoid him as much as possible. Things were just too awkward between them.

The server arrived and they ordered the burger special, then she excused herself to visit the ladies' room. She was washing her hands and studying her face in the mirror, wondering if she should bother to touch up her makeup when she felt a tug on her trousers. She looked down to see an adorable little blonde girl looking up at her. "Can you lift me up so I can wash my hands?" the girl asked.

"Well, sure." Harper dried her own hands, then grasped the child around the waist and boosted her up until she could reach the sink. "Do you need help turning on the water?" she asked, though how she was going to manage while she was holding the child, she couldn't imagine.

"I can do it," the little girl said, and twisted the handle of the faucet. She pumped soap, then scrubbed vigorously, a look of deep concentration on her face.

"You're doing a great job," Harper said. Such tiny hands, though she was a sturdy child, heavier than Harper might have thought, dressed in a pink ruffled dress and jeans with a hole in one knee, a pink ribbon coming loose from her hair. She leaned closer and caught a whiff of strawberry shampoo. A rush of tenderness almost overwhelmed her.

"Okay, I'm ready to dry now."

Harper set the child on her feet and handed her a paper towel from the dispenser on the wall. The girl very carefully dried each finger, then crumpled the paper towel and deposited it in the trash.

"Is there anyone named Charlotte in here?" a woman called from the door.

"That's me!" The little girl stuck up her hand as if she'd been called on in class.

The woman smiled. "Your dad asked me to check on you," she said. "He's getting a little nervous out here."

"Okay." Charlotte turned to Harper. "You need to come meet my dad."

Who was Harper to argue with a command like this? Curious, she followed her new friend into the hallway outside the restrooms.

And stopped. Because of course, she should have known this was coming. If she had learned nothing else the past few years, it was that the universe had a definite sense of irony. "This lady helped me wash my hands," Charlotte was saying, holding up both hands as if for inspection.

"Hello again, Ryker," Harper said

"Hello, Harper." He had exchanged his uniform for jeans and a T-shirt that did a good job of showing off his chest and biceps. The Ryker she had known before had definitely not been this pumped. "Thanks for helping my girl."

My girl. The affection behind the words brought a lump to her throat. He rested one hand on Charlotte's shoulder as she leaned back against his legs, her gaze shifting between them, bright and expectant. "I was happy to help."

"This is Charlotte," he said. "In case she didn't introduce herself."

Harper forced her attention to the child. She could see a little of Ryker in the broad forehead and something about the eyes. But the rest of her must take after her mother. Christine had said Ryker was a single dad, so what had happened to Charlotte's mother? "It's nice to meet you," she said. "I'm Harper."

"I never knew anyone named Harper before," Charlotte said. She grabbed Ryker's hand and swung on it. "Can we eat pizza now?"

"Would you like to join us?" he asked.

Was that hope she saw in his eyes? Or was he merely being polite? "I'm with friends," she said. "And I already ordered."

"Sure." He took a step back, his expression unreadable. "I'll let you get to it."

Maybe some other time, she should have said. Or even *I'd love to catch up with you.*

Oh, what was the point? She and Ryker were over and done with and had been for years. The sooner she accepted that, the better.

She headed back toward her booth but hadn't gone far before someone grabbed her arm. Startled, she found herself face-to-face with a petite woman with a halo of messy blond hair. The woman's long nails dug into the skin of Harper's forearm. "What were you doing with that little girl?" the woman demanded. She had very blue eyes, fringed with long false lashes, and her gaze bored into Harper.

Harper wrenched away from her. "Who are you?" she asked.

"I saw you in the ladies' room with that little girl. What were you doing with her?"

"I was taking her to her father. Her father, the sheriff's deputy."

Harper had hoped the mention of a cop would make the woman back off, but she only laughed. "I know all about Ryker," she said. "He should keep a better eye on his kid." She turned and walked away, leaving by the fire door at the end of the hallway.

Harper stared after her. Should she say something to

Ryker about the strange woman? But what would she say? Some nosy woman thinks you shouldn't let your little girl go to the bathroom by herself? He had stood outside the door waiting for Charlotte, and even sent someone in to check on her. What else could a dad do?

She moved to the fire door and pushed it open enough to look out. No sign of the woman. She was probably just a local busybody. Better to leave it.

"I was beginning to think we were going to have to send out a search party," Christine said when Harper returned to their booth. "Your burger is getting cold."

"I ran into someone who wanted to talk." She popped a french fry into her mouth, hoping to forestall conversation.

"Is that a bruise on your arm?"

Harper followed Grace's gaze to the four round dark spots forming on her arm. She could still feel that woman's fingers digging into her, her gaze searing. But she didn't want to talk about that. Because talking about the woman would mean talking about Ryker, and she wasn't ready for that. Not yet. "I wonder how that happened," she said, and went back to eating her burger.

THE NEXT MORNING, Ryker reported to the sheriff's department for a mandatory meeting of all personnel. He filled his coffee cup from the carafe at the back of the conference room and greeted some of his fellow officers, then took a seat along one side of the long table. It had felt strange at first, being in this place that held no good memories for him. He had had pretty much zero interactions with law enforcement until Aiden had been kidnapped. Then they had questioned him repeatedly, making it clear he was their chief suspect. Even though they had eventually cleared him, his life hadn't been the same since. Back then he never would have dreamed he would end up on this side of the law.

A lot had changed in the seven years since his arrest. Sheriff Travis Walker, only in his early thirties but recently reelected—having run unopposed—sat at the head of the table, flanked by his brother Sergeant Gage Walker on one side, and Deputy Dwight Prentice on the other.

Ryker looked around the table at his fellow officers, some he knew better than others. They were a fairly young lot, typical of a small department. Many of them, like him, had young children. Travis had nine-month-old twins— a boy and a girl—while Gage had a six-month-old baby girl as well as a seven-year-old daughter. Jamie Douglas, the only female deputy, had a three-month-old daughter. Dwight Prentice and his wife had no children. Declan Owen had been the newest recruit until Ryker was hired, though he had more experience than most of them, having worked for the US Marshals Service. Shane Ellis, Chris DelRay and Wes Landry rounded out the force, along with a few reserve officers who filled in during vacations, illnesses or emergencies.

"Let's get started," Travis said, and the hum of conversation died down. "We've had a string of vandalism incidents in the high country. Someone stole some metal roofing the Historical Society had purchased to stabilize the old mine boarding house up at the Mary Simmons Mine. Maybe the same person or persons took a dozen two-by-fours the owners of a mining claim off Iron Springs Road had purchased to build a storage shed on the property."

"Dale Perkins stopped me last week to complain about people camping illegally at his place," Dwight said. "I told them if he caught them in the act we could charge them with trespassing, but he said since he doesn't live up there, that's hard to do. He was most upset about all the trash they leave behind."

"Illegal camping increases the danger of a campfire getting out of hand," Jamie said. "People who ignore private property signs won't necessarily comply with fire regulations, either."

"It might be transients," Gage said.

"Whoever this is doesn't seem to be moving on," Travis said. "Keep your eyes and ears open around town, and if you get a chance to patrol some of the roads leading into the high country, do so."

The meeting moved on to cover the need for traffic control during a Jeep rally in the town park the upcoming weekend, preparations for Independence Day celebrations the next month, a firearms training session in two weeks and a reminder to turn in reports on time. "Adelaide says if she gets any incomplete reports, she will come looking for you," Travis said.

Nervous laughter circled the table. Ryker had already learned that Office Manager Adelaide Kinkaid was not someone he wanted to cross. She didn't have to raise her voice to make him feel like an errant schoolboy.

The meeting broke up and Ryker gathered his belongings. He had a few free hours until he reported for his shift at three. "How's it going, Ryker?" Gage asked.

Travis's younger brother was more outgoing than his sibling and served as a de facto training officer for the new recruits. Even though Ryker wasn't a true rookie, having worked four and a half years with the police department in Longmont, Colorado, he was still settling into the routine here in Eagle Mountain. "It's going well," Ryker said. When he had interviewed for the job here, he had been upfront about his past experiences with the department. Having grown up in Eagle Mountain, Travis and Gage knew Aiden's case, and made it clear they considered it irrelevant to Ryker's hiring. Which it was. He tossed his coffee cup into the trash.

"How's Charlotte doing at Robin's Nest Day Care?" Gage asked.

"She's doing well. She likes her teacher and is making friends." Not that Charlotte ever had problems making friends.

Gage leaned back against the counter beside the coffee machine. "Maya and I are thinking about enrolling our youngest there in a few months when Maya goes back to teaching school," he said.

"If we all keep having more babies, we could open a department day care." Jamie squeezed past Ryker to refill her travel mug with coffee.

"Who's watching your little one?" Gage asked.

"My neighbor. She's helped with Donna for years, and she seemed thrilled to add a baby to the mix." She glanced at Ryker. "Donna is my sister. She has Down's and is pretty independent, but it's good to have someone around she can call on when Nate or I are working."

"Nate's a ranger with the forest service," Gage said, filling in yet another detail to help Ryker form a complete picture of his coworkers.

"Thank goodness he works a set schedule," Jamie said. "That makes it a lot easier to manage care."

"My mom and dad are a big help with Charlotte," Ryker said. "It's the main reason I moved back to Eagle Mountain. I don't know how I'd look after her without them."

"This is a great place to raise a family," Gage said.

"Says the man who's never lived anywhere else," Jamie said.

"Doesn't make it any less true." Gage turned back to

Ryker. "If you need anything, let one of us know. On or off the job. That's what we're here for."

"Thanks." But Ryker was unlikely to ask. It had been hard enough turning to his parents for help after Kim left.

He was halfway across the parking lot to his car when his phone rang. "Hey, Mom," he answered, as he hit the key fob to unlock the door.

"Ryker, is Charlotte with you?"

The panic in his mother's voice stopped Ryker cold. "Charlotte is at day care. I dropped her off this morning before my meeting."

"She was there, but she isn't now. The director just called to ask if one of us had checked her out without telling anyone. I told her we would never do that."

"What do they mean, she isn't there? She couldn't have disappeared." His heart beat painfully and he fought a wave of nausea.

"She went out with the other kids in her class for morning playtime. The teachers were with them—two of them." His mother sounded more in control. She had always been good in a crisis. "A little boy fell and they thought he had broken his arm. They were tending to him and when they called everyone to come back inside, Charlotte wasn't there. Sheila Lindstrom said she looked everywhere. They even checked the houses near the day care, thinking Charlotte might have gone to visit someone there. You know how friendly she is. But she wasn't there. Ryker, what are we going to do?"

His first instinct was to go to the day care center—to tear the place apart if he had to, looking for his daughter. Maybe she was hiding, and she had fallen asleep. Or they had overlooked her somehow.

But the cold black knot in the center of his chest told

him that hadn't happened. Sheila and the others would have thought of those things. "Just sit tight, Mom," he said. "I'll take care of it." He pocketed his phone and hurried back into the sheriff's department. This couldn't be happening again. Not his little girl.

A group of deputies were gathered around Gage and Travis outside the conference room. They looked up as he burst inside. "My daughter is missing," he announced. "Someone's taken Charlotte."

Chapter Three

Harper had just settled into lettering the ski trail map when Devlin Anderson, a talented young artist who had a penchant for vintage menswear, swept into the studio. Today he wore the pants and vest from a brown plaid suit, with brown wing tips and a brown bow tie. But his normally neat hair was ruffled, and he was red in the face, as if he'd been running. "I was down the street getting a latte when I heard there's a little girl missing," he said. "They're asking for volunteers to help with the search."

Chairs scraped and paper rustled as people rose from their worktables. "Who's missing?"

"When?"

"From where?"

The owner of the business, Patterson Taylor, emerged from his office. "What's going on?"

"There's a little girl missing," Devlin said. "We need to help look."

"Who is she?" Harper asked.

"All I know is her name is Charlotte," Devlin said. "She's four years old with long blond hair. She's wearing a pink-checked sundress and she disappeared from Robin's Nest Day Care. You know, that cute little house over on Second Street."

"Charlotte Vernon?" Harper didn't know her voice could squeak like that.

"Do you know her?" Another coworker, Lisa, rushed over to take Harper's arm. "You'd better sit down. You look like you're going to faint."

Harper straightened and forced herself to breathe deeply. "I'm okay," she said. "But I need to go help." Poor Charlotte. Poor Ryker! He must be frantic.

"They're asking volunteers to assemble in front of the sheriff's department," Devlin said. "They'll give us instructions."

Harper's text alert sounded and she studied the message. "You sure you're okay?" Lisa asked.

Harper nodded. "It's search and rescue. They're asking for search volunteers also."

The office emptied out as everyone hurried two blocks over to the sheriff's department. The sidewalks were filled with others headed in the same direction. Harper spotted SAR volunteer Carrie Andrews, an architect whose office was nearby and moved to join her. Hannah Richards and her mother, Brit, from the Alpiner Inn several streets over, soon gathered with them.

Sheriff Travis Walker asked for silence, then read out Charlotte's description. Four years old. Thirty-eight inches tall. Thirty-eight pounds. Blond hair, blue eyes. Pink sundress and shorts. Pink sneakers. "She's been missing less than an hour," he said. "Sheriff's deputies will search nearby homes. I'm asking civilian volunteers to search alleys, backyards, vacant lots. Look anywhere a small child might hide. It's possible she fell asleep or was hurt. Behind dumpsters, in tall grass—look everywhere. If you find anything, call for help and wait for others to assist."

Harper studied the faces of the deputies gathered around the sheriff, their expressions grim. She didn't see Ryker. Was he inside the station? Or somewhere else, already searching for his daughter?

Wherever he was, he was probably beside himself. In the few moments she had seen them together, there had been no mistaking the love he had for his daughter. And after what he had been through when Aiden was taken—people had said some terrible things, and even after it was proven he couldn't have been the one to hurt the boy, there were still whispers. Harper's parents had been quick to condemn him, and they hadn't been alone.

Search and rescue volunteers split into two teams, assigned to search a condo development under construction a few blocks from the day care. The site was full of potential hazards for a small child, from broken glass and jagged nails to an open basement. Upon hearing the situation, the construction workers pitched in to help. They formed a line to move through the site, turning over sheets of plywood and peering into any cavity. No one said anything, but Harper sensed that, like her, they were steeling themselves for the sight of a small body, injured in a fall or crushed by a piece of lumber. There were so many ways a small child was vulnerable, and she could see how a place like this might be tempting for an adventurous little girl.

Charlotte had struck her as the curious type, her big blue eyes looking into Harper's without fear. Harper remembered the weight of her as she lifted her to the sink, and the strawberry scent of her hair, so sweet and innocent. Obviously Charlotte wasn't the first little girl she had encountered in the past seven years. But she was the first who had affected her so viscerally.

Because she was Ryker's. Because she made Harper think of their little girl. Would she have been like Charlotte if she had lived?

Seven years ago

"CAN'T I STAY up and watch TV with you?"

"Sorry, bud. Your mom was really clear that your bedtime is eight." Ryker patted his little cousin's shoulder. Aiden was small for his age, with a cowlick that stuck up at the back of his head no matter how much his mother, Melissa, tried to plaster it down. He had recently lost a tooth and the gap gave him a particularly rascally look when he grinned, as he did a lot. He was a happy kid, and even though he whined about having to go to bed, he obediently climbed under the sheets. "Did you brush your teeth?" Ryker asked.

"Yeah." Aiden looked toward the window beside his bed. "Can you leave the blinds up? I like to look out until I get sleepy."

"Okay. I'll be just down the hall if you need anything."

Ryker shut the bedroom door and walked down the hall to the living room. He turned the television on, keeping the sound low, and flipped through the channels, looking for something to hold his interest. He thought about calling Harper, but her parents didn't let her have her own phone, so he would have to call their home phone, and her mom was liable to answer. Mrs. Stanick had made it clear she didn't like Ryker, though he couldn't figure out why. Yes, he had a motorcycle, but that didn't mean he was dangerous or anything.

He settled on an episode of *Deadwood* and lay back on the sofa, a pillow under his head. He had gotten up early to finish an essay for English class and found himself drifting off.

When he woke, the show was over and it was dark outside. He sat up and checked the time. Nine o'clock. He went to the bathroom, then moved to the end of the hall and eased open the door to Aiden's room. He expected to find the little guy sleeping, but instead the bed was empty, the covers thrown back, half-trailing on the floor.

"Aiden?" Ryker stepped into the room. He looked around the small space and started toward the closet, but a rattling noise stopped him. The window was wide open, a breeze knocking the top of the blinds against the frame.

"Aiden!" Ryker rushed to the window. The screen was missing. He stuck his head out and could just make it out, lying on the ground. "Aiden!" He stared down at the screen—six feet down. A long way for a little boy to drop. And there was no sign of the boy anywhere.

Heart pounding, he raced outside. "Aiden!" he shouted. "Aiden, where are you?"

He ran around to the side of the house. No sign of the boy. No sign of anyone.

"Ryker? Is everything okay?"

He turned and saw Mrs. Kenner, a retired teacher who lived across the street, on her front porch. He jogged toward her. "Have you seen Aiden?" he asked.

She frowned, and pulled her robe—faded pink and quilted—more closely around her. "No, I haven't seen Aiden. Isn't it a little late for him to be out?"

"I put him to bed at eight and when I went to check on him just now, he wasn't there." He looked back toward the house, hoping to see the little boy pop out from behind the shrubbery or a dark corner of the yard. "His window is open and he isn't there."

"Where could he have gone?" Mrs. Kenner didn't look upset, merely puzzled. "Do you think he's hiding from you?"

"I don't know," Ryker said. "He's just…gone."

Mrs. Kenner put her hand on his arm. "Then maybe you'd better call someone."

He nodded, and groped in the pocket of his jeans for his phone. He stared at it for a long moment, wondering who to call. Not Aiden's mom. Melissa would faint if she thought something happened to her little boy. Aiden's dad was at work, and Ryker didn't know that number. He dialed a number he knew by heart. His father answered on the second ring. "Ryker? Is everything okay?"

"Aiden is missing," he said. "I went to check his bedroom and he's just…gone." He felt cold all over, and started to shake.

"CAN YOU THINK of any place Charlotte might have gone to? A friend she might have decided to visit? A store she liked and wanted to see again?" Declan Owen sat with Ryker in the sheriff's office, conducting what passed for a formal interview. Ryker wondered if the sheriff had assigned Declan this duty because, like Ryker, he was new to the department. Or because of his experience with the US Marshals Service. Or maybe it was because Declan didn't have children of his own. It didn't take a particularly perceptive person to see how Charlotte's disappearance had hit hard among the many officers in the department who were parents of young children.

"I don't think she wandered off from the day care," Ryker said. "She wouldn't have any reason to do that. I think someone took her." He closed his eyes, willing himself to keep it together. Charlotte wasn't Aiden. What had happened to him wouldn't necessarily happen to her.

"Why do you think that?" Declan asked. "You've taught her not to go with strangers, right?"

That was basic parenting 101, especially for a cop. Despite the way Charlotte had apparently enlisted Harper, a stranger to her, for help in the ladies' room, he didn't think his little girl would let someone she didn't know talk her into leaving the day care. They had even playacted scenarios where someone tried to tell Charlotte her daddy was hurt or they had a puppy they needed her to see. Charlotte had practiced saying *no* and going to get an adult for help. "This wouldn't have been a stranger," he said, and the certainty behind those words edged out some of the stark fear.

Declan leaned toward him. "Who do you think took her?" he asked.

"Her mother. My ex-wife." Was he saying that because he believed it to be true, or merely because he wanted it to be true? He wet his lips and said, "Charlotte wouldn't go with a stranger, but she would probably go with her mother. Even though she hasn't seen Kim in years, she has a picture of her mother in her room and she talks about her."

Declan nodded. He would be familiar with the same statistics as Ryker—the vast majority of kidnapped children were taken by a relative, often the noncustodial parent. "Has your ex-wife threatened to take Charlotte with her? Have the two of you argued over custody?"

"Kim hasn't seen Charlotte in three years," Ryker said. "Not since she packed up and moved out of the house to live with another man. When I filed for divorce and asked for full custody, she didn't argue. She's never even attempted to visit Charlotte."

"Then why do you think she would take her now?" Declan asked.

How to explain how Kim's mind worked? Not that Ryker

would ever be an expert, but two years of living with her had lent him insights he didn't necessarily want. "Kim is impulsive. And self-centered. When she wants something, she wants it now and will run over anyone who tries to keep her from getting her way. She was also very influenced by her boyfriend. If he decided he wanted them to have Charlotte, Kim wouldn't bother with petitioning for custody through the courts. She would storm in and take what she wanted—her daughter. I think that's what she's done now." His stomach churned at the idea, but he could so clearly see it happening. Charlotte hadn't seen her mother since she was thirteen months old, but she had never forgotten her. In the beginning, Ryker had believed that Kim would change her mind and want to see her little girl, so he had kept pictures of Kim and Charlotte together, and when Charlotte asked questions about her mother, he tried to answer honestly, without making Charlotte feel that her mother's abandonment was in any way her fault.

So Charlotte would probably have recognized Kim if she approached. And if Kim had urged Charlotte to come with her, she probably would have obeyed. What little girl wouldn't want to go with her mother? Especially when her mother was beautiful and petite, and bore a more than passing resemblance to the fairy godmothers in the picture books Charlotte loved.

"Have you had any contact with your ex-wife in the past few months?" Declan asked. "Do you know where she's been living?"

"The last I heard, she was still with Mick and they were living out east of Denver, in Gilcrest." He shifted in the chair. "I haven't spoken to Kim in more than three years. The divorce was negotiated through our lawyers and we were never in the same room after she packed up and moved out. But I've kept tabs on her over the years." Given Mick's criminal history, Ryker had felt safer knowing what he and Kim were up to.

"Do you think she's still with the man she left with?" Declan asked.

"I don't know for sure. Maybe." He shifted, uncomfortable. If Kim was still with Mick, she had stayed with him almost twice as long as she had been with Ryker. But he could see it. Kim hadn't just loved Mick, she had been enthralled with him. Under his sway.

"What's this man's name?"

"Michael Davis. He goes by Mick. If you look him up, you'll see he has a record."

One of Declan's eyebrows twitched, but it was the only tell that this surprised him. "Has he served time?" he asked. "For what crimes?"

"Drugs. Extortion. Fraud. Theft."

"Nice guy."

"Oh yeah." He blew out a breath. "Kim said she wanted someone who wasn't like me. I took it as a compliment."

"I'll pull his record, see if I can get a recent photo," Declan said. "Does your ex have any priors?"

"Not unless they've happened since the divorce. When I met her she was squeaky clean. I made the mistake of believing she was ordinary."

Declan stood and rested a hand on his shoulder. "We'll put out an APB on your ex. We've already issued an Amber Alert for Charlotte. We're knocking on doors around the day care, trying to find anyone who might have seen someone talking to Charlotte. And most of the town is out looking for her."

He left the room and Ryker collapsed forward, elbows on his knees, head in his hands, fighting back tears and a terror that threatened to overwhelm him. Charlotte had to be all right. His beautiful girl had to be all right. He prayed she was with Kim. The woman might be irresponsible and misguided and a hundred other adjectives that added up to someone he could never trust. But she wouldn't hurt her child. She wouldn't let Mick hurt her child.

She wouldn't. He had to hold on to that belief.

THE SEARCH FOR Charlotte Vernon ceased when it became too dark to see. By that time more than two hundred people had combed every inch of the town and found no sign of the little girl. Too upset to go home to an empty apartment, Harper gathered with her fellow search and rescue volunteers at their headquarters, where they sat at the long tables used for training and watched television reports about the missing girl, her picture filling the screen, sometimes alone, sometimes with her father.

"I feel so sorry for Ryker," Hannah said. "Jake says he's holding up okay, and they're all rallying around to support him and his parents, but I just know he's sick about this."

"Shh. Who's that?" The question, from someone at the other end of the table, directed their attention to the television. A different picture filled the screen, of a woman with abundant blond hair and blue eyes.

A second picture took its place—Ryker and the woman together, the woman holding a baby. "Kimberley 'Kim' Rhodes Vernon, who may also be going by the name Kim Davis, is wanted for questioning in the disappearance of her daughter, Charlotte Vernon. A woman who was passing the day care facility about the time of Charlotte's disappearance reported seeing a blond woman—who may have been Kim Vernon—with the girl on the sidewalk in front of the day care."

The image on the screen changed to one of a man, thinning blond hair in a single braid, heavy eyebrows and a blond moustache, a flag tattoo on one bare arm, an eagle on the front of the T-shirt. "Ms. Vernon may be in the company of this man, Michael or Mick Davis. If you see either of these people, especially in the company of a little girl, please notify the police."

Harper shoved back her chair and stood. Hannah stared up at her. "Are you okay?"

"I need to talk to the sheriff," she said. "I saw that woman."

"When?"

"Today?"

"Where did you see her?" The questions came from all sides. Harper shook her head. "She was at Mo's last night. I need to tell the sheriff."

No one tried to stop her as she hurried outside to her car. She forced herself to slow down and pay attention to the road as she drove to the sheriff's department.

The parking lot at the sheriff's department was full and at least a dozen people milled about outside, from curious locals and tourists to a few reporters. Harper pushed through the door and found the lobby even more crowded. She made her way to the desk at the back of the room, where an older woman with purple-framed bifocals regarded her with tired eyes. Her name tag read Adelaide. "May I help you?"

"I need to see the sheriff," Harper said. She lowered her voice, not wanting any reporters nearby to hear. "I saw Kim Vernon. Yesterday, at Mo's."

Adelaide stood. "Come with me."

Harper followed the older woman through a door and down a long hallway to a cramped office. Sheriff Walker stood when they entered the room. Ryker, slumped in a chair in front of the sheriff's desk, looked up at her with red-rimmed eyes. "This woman says she saw Kim Vernon yesterday," Adelaide announced.

Ryker shot out of his chair. "Where did you see her?" he asked. "Was she alone? Are you sure it was her?"

"Sit down, please. Harper, isn't it?" asked the sheriff.

She sat on a folding chair and scooted it closer to the desk, within inches of Ryker. He sat down and stared at her, hands gripping his knees. "Harper Stanick," she said.

The sheriff pulled a yellow legal pad toward him and took a pen from a cup on his desk. "Tell me what you saw."

She told him about her conversation with the woman she was sure was Kim Vernon, outside the restroom at Mo's Pub the night before. "She said I should keep a better eye on my kid?" Ryker's deep voice held even more gravel than usual. "Why didn't you tell me about this?"

"I didn't think it meant anything," Harper protested. "She was just some nosy woman."

"You say she left out the fire door?" Travis prompted.

"Yes. There's a door at the end of the hallway that goes out into the parking lot."

"Did you see what kind of vehicle she was driving?" Ryker asked. "Was she with anyone else?"

"No. I didn't see into the parking lot." She turned to Ryker. "I'm so sorry about Charlotte. But if she was taken by her mother, surely she wouldn't hurt her."

The tight lines around his eyes didn't ease, but he nodded. "No, I don't think she would hurt her."

"Thank you for coming forward with this information," Travis said. "We appreciate it."

She stood, and was surprised when Ryker rose also. "I'll walk you out," he said.

In the hallway, he touched her arm. "Let's go out the

back," he said, and pointed down the hall. "Less likely to see reporters."

She waited while he badged through the door lock, and they stepped out into what was apparently the employee lot, black-and-white sheriff's department SUVs interspersed with other vehicles. Moths flitted around the security lights, but beyond where they stood, all was dark and quiet. The chill common to nights in the mountains, even in summer, had also descended, and Harper tried not to think about Charlotte without a sweater in the cold.

"How are your parents doing?" she asked. She didn't know Wanda and Steve Vernon very well, but she remembered them being nice people. Much nicer to her than her parents had been to Ryker.

"They're taking it hard. Especially my mom. She's spent a lot of time with Charlotte since we moved here." He sighed. "I was floundering on my own, trying to work shifts at the police department and find childcare. When my mom suggested I move back home I resisted the idea at first, but it ended up being a lifesaver. I think it's better for Charlotte, too, having my folks around."

"I'm glad you have their support now, too," she said.

"I didn't mean to jump down your throat just now," Ryker said, not looking at her. "There was no reason you should have mentioned seeing Kim to me. You didn't know her, and it's not like she really did or said anything threatening."

"How long were you married?" She wanted to take the question back as soon as she said it. Of all the things to ask at a time like this, that wasn't one of them. It was none of her business anyway.

"Less than two years," he said. "It was a bad idea from the start but we had only been dating about six weeks when she found out she was pregnant, and I wanted to do the right thing." He did look at her then, eyes dark and shadowed. "I would have married you, you know."

"I know." She blew out a deep breath. "But my parents were right. I mean, about us being too young. That wouldn't have been a good way to start out." She had been seventeen. He had just turned eighteen, in their senior year of high school.

"Would you have waited for me?" he asked.

"Yes." She didn't have to think about the answer.

"Then I'm sorry I didn't wait for you. I figured you felt the same way about me your parents did."

When Harper's parents had learned she was pregnant, and that Ryker was the father, they had been beyond furious. When Aiden had disappeared only a few days later, they had been even more set against him. They sent Harper to Florida, where she was to live with her mother's sister, Florence, until she delivered the baby.

"You know they sent me to Florida, right?" she said. "They took away my computer and my phone. My aunt wouldn't let me out of her sight. It was like being in prison." A posh prison, with its own pool and beach access. But she had been miserable without him.

"I didn't know about that until later. You had just vanished." He glanced at her again. "I even had some wild idea they might have harmed you. Your mother was so furious, the one time I tried to talk to her."

"You talked to her?" Harper felt her eyes go wide at the idea.

"Yeah. She told me she wasn't going to see her only child's life ruined and while you were upset with her now, you would thank her later for preventing you from making a huge mistake. Awful as they were, her words gave me hope. Leaving hadn't been your idea."

She pictured him, trying to be a tough guy, but really still a boy. Hurt and probably angry and more than a little lost. She had felt all those things, too. "I'm sorry," she said. "I wish I could have at least said goodbye to you, and explained what was going on."

"It was a long time before I found out you lost the baby," he said. "A friend of yours told me. I don't think she knew I was the father."

She stared at him. "I wrote you a letter," she said. "You didn't get it?"

"No. But I moved away the week after graduation." He stared off across the parking lot.

"What a mess we both were."

"Yeah, well. I met Kim three years later and we got involved and that was a mess, too. Except for Charlotte. It was all worth it for her."

She did what she had been wanting to do all night then, and tucked her hand into the crook of his arm and leaned against him. "You're going to find her," she said. "You've got so many people looking for her and Kim—she's a striking-looking woman, isn't she? The kind who stands out. And Charlotte is such a beautiful kid. People will notice her, too."

He didn't say anything. Maybe he didn't believe the words. As a cop, he had probably seen and heard all kinds of horrible things that happened to missing kids. And then there was Aiden. His killer had never been found. She was grateful she didn't have those things in her head. "Thanks for your help tonight," he said. "And I know you and the other search and rescue volunteers looked for her today."

"She's a terrific kid," Harper said. "She won me over right away."

"She does that. I don't know where she gets it from." He unwound her hand from his arm and took a step away. "I'd better get back in there," he said. "Thanks again."

I'm not going to cry, she told herself as she walked around to the front of the building where she had left her car. She had spent so many years imagining what their reunion might be like—how they would exchange their stories and maybe laugh at the mistakes they had made. In her imagination it had never been like this—the facts laid out but so much left unsaid. And the heavy weight of sadness over his missing child threatening to pull them under.

She got into her car and started it, but sat for a long moment, the tears in her eyes blurring the world around her like raindrops on a window.

Chapter Four

Ryker left the sheriff's department an hour after Harper. The search for Charlotte was paused until first light, and while the sheriff had sent another bulletin alerting all law enforcement agencies to be on the lookout for Kim, there was little hope of a response until the next day. Wherever Kim and Charlotte were, they were probably sleeping.

He was walking toward his truck when a man on the sidewalk called his name. He looked up and was surprised to see a gray-haired man hobbling toward him. The man moved quickly, despite the fact that one shoulder was hunched and he moved with an awkward, sideways gait. He stopped in front of Ryker and a nearby streetlight illuminated a weathered, deeply lined face. "Any news about your little girl?" the man asked.

Ryker shook his head. The man didn't look like a reporter. He wore dirty jeans and a red-checked flannel shirt with a rip in one sleeve. "I was one of the searchers today," the man said. "I wanted to do what I could to help."

"Thank you," Ryker said. "I appreciate it."

The man looked around them, at the deserted street, lined with silent and closed businesses. "It seems strange to be out here doing this again. I helped looked for your cousin, too."

Ryker stared. "What is your name?"

"Gary. Gary Langley." He held up a hand, the fingers knotted and twisted. "I'd offer to shake hands but I can't anymore. I had an accident at work just about a year after your cousin went missing, caused a lot of neurological damage. I've been on full disability ever since. But something like this, I like to get out and do what I can."

"Thanks." Ryker took a step back. "Is there something in particular you wanted?"

"No. I was just hoping for news. I hope you find her soon. It's terrible the things that can happen to a child these days."

He turned and shuffled away. Ryker stared after him. Had the man reminded him about Aiden on purpose, perhaps with the goal of unsettling him? If so, he had succeeded. Not that Aiden's disappearance and death had been far from his mind all day.

He shook his head and continued walking to his truck and drove home. His mother met him at the back door, eyes full of unasked questions. He shook his head. "No news."

"Nothing?" Wanda followed him into the kitchen. The room smelled of coffee and lemon dish detergent, the black granite countertops reflecting pools of overhead light. "I can't believe no one has seen her," Wanda said.

"I'm sure she's with Kim," Ryker said. "Harper Stanick came in and said she ran into a woman who fit Kim's description at Mo's last night. Kim had seen Harper with Charlotte in the ladies' room and asked what she was doing with her."

"Harper was with Charlotte in the ladies' room?" Wanda looked puzzled.

"I had to send Charlotte into the ladies' room by herself. She won't go into the men's room with me anymore, and it's not really appropriate, anyway. She couldn't reach the sink to wash her hands, so she asked Harper for help."

"We've told her not to talk to strangers."

"We've also told her how important it is to wash her hands. Anyway, I guess she figured Harper was trustworthy. And Harper brought her right out to me."

"How is Harper? I didn't know she was back in town." Unlike the Stanicks, Wanda had welcomed Harper into her home. While she hadn't been happy about the news that her son's not-yet-eighteen-year-old girlfriend was going to have a baby, she had adopted a positive attitude and promised to help as much as possible. When Harper had disappeared from their lives, Ryker had come to believe his mother had mourned almost as much as he had. After all, Harper's baby would have been her first grandchild.

"She's okay, I guess," he said. "She looks good. She's volunteering with search and rescue. I ran into her when I worked that accident Tuesday—the one with the baby in the car seat." Was that really only two days ago? It seemed a lifetime.

"You didn't say."

"Yeah, well." There were a lot of things he didn't tell his mom.

"What did Kim say to Harper?" Wanda asked.

"She wanted to know what she was doing with Charlotte. Then she said…she said I needed to do a better job of watching my kid." His voice cracked and he had to turn away. He didn't want to break down. Not just because he didn't want his mother to see him that way, but because he was afraid if he started sobbing, he wouldn't be able to stop. He had to keep it together. His parents needed him to do that. And Charlotte needed him, too. When she was found—and he had to believe she would be found—he was going to be there, not in a heap somewhere crying.

He felt something warm on his back. His mother's hand rubbing up and down, the way she had when he was a boy. "You're a good father," she said. "The best. Charlotte knows that. You didn't do anything wrong. This is all on Kim. To be honest, I'm relieved to know Kim is probably with her, instead of some stranger who might harm her."

He nodded. Instead of some stranger like the one who had harmed Aiden. He turned to face her again. Maybe the best way to get through this horror was to shift into cop mode. Focus on the job. "We put out an APB for Kim and Mick, and we're trying to find any vehicles registered to them. Maybe somebody will spot them."

"Somebody will spot them," his mother echoed. She stepped back. "I saved dinner for you. It's chicken soup. I thought that might be easiest to get down."

He shook his head. "I couldn't eat."

She opened her mouth and he knew she was going to urge him to eat, but she apparently thought better of it. "Then try to get some sleep," she said. "Tomorrow is going to be another long day."

RYKER SPENT A restless night, drifting to sleep, then waking to the remembrance that Charlotte was gone. He fought back thoughts of all the worst things that could happen to her, managing to doze again, only to come fully awake just after six to pale light showing behind the bedroom shades. He stared at that light and wondered if Charlotte was seeing it, too. Where was she? She was such a part of him now— how could he not know where she was?

But she wasn't in control of where she went—Kim and Mick were. And they were unknown to him. He tried to think of everything Kim had told him about Mick that might be relevant. When she left it had been all about Mick and what Mick wanted, and he didn't think that would change. Mick wanted to be free. He wanted to live by his own rules. He wanted to go somewhere and live off the land and look after himself. Kim was all in. They were going to create their own little paradise together.

And what about Charlotte? Kim had fallen silent for a long minute when Ryker had asked this question. "Once Mick and I get our place built, she can come see us," she said. "Until then, she might as well stay with you. We're probably going to be traveling around for a while, looking for the right place, and that's hard with a little kid."

"You would just abandon your daughter this way?" Ryker asked.

"I'm not abandoning her. I'll be back when I have a place for her."

"That's not going to happen," Ryker said. "If you turn your back on her now, she will never live with you again. I'll see to it."

He wanted to frighten her into doing the right thing. Not that he wanted her to stay with them. He had known months before this moment that their marriage was over. But Charlotte adored her mother, and she deserved to have two loving parents. He wasn't going to let Kim hurt their daughter this way.

But Kim wasn't frightened. She even had the nerve to smile. "Oh Ryker, I'm her mother," she said. "Of course she'll live with me again, when the time is right."

He had to leave the room then. The urge to lash out at Kim was so strong it frightened him. He went into Charlotte's nursery and held the baby until he heard Kim and Mick drive away.

Kim didn't contest the divorce or the custody arrangement. He lost touch with her and after a couple of years, he had begun to believe she was out of their lives for good.

But somehow she had found them here in Eagle Mountain. Did that mean she and Mick had established their homestead and she was claiming what she thought of as hers? Never mind that she was a stranger to Charlotte and didn't know anything about her, from what she liked to eat to her favorite books and what childhood illnesses she had suffered. What Kim wanted, Kim took.

He showered and shaved, and dressed in his uniform. Travis had told him he was on family leave until Charlotte was found but if he was going to spend the day at the sheriff's department, he wanted to look like he belonged there.

He was drinking his first cup of coffee when his phone rang. When he saw the sheriff's name on the screen, he scrambled to answer, his hands shaking. "The FBI is coming in this morning to interview you," Travis said. "They say they have some information but they wouldn't tell me on the phone what it was."

Right. It made sense to call in the feds for a child abduction. "I'll be right there," Ryker said.

His mother didn't say anything when he told her he had to go to a meeting at the sheriff's department, but she shoved a travel cup into his hand. "It's a smoothie with protein powder," she said. "Drink it even if you don't want to. You're no good to anyone if you don't eat."

He felt better after he drank the smoothie. Strong enough to face the feds, anyway. Travis was waiting in his office, pressed and polished as ever, though the shadows under his eyes suggested he hadn't slept much better than Ryker. Was he thinking about what it would be like to have one of his children taken?

Special Agents Guy Cussler and Adam Reno shook hands with Ryker when Travis introduced them, then the four men gathered around the conference table. "We've had a report of a couple with a little girl matching the descriptions of your daughter and Kimberly and Mick Davis at a campground just outside of Utah last night," Agent Cussler said. "Unfortunately, by the time authorities arrived at the campground this morning, they were gone. But we now know they've traveled into Utah, so we'll be pursuing the case from there."

"Do you know of any connection they have to anyone in Utah?" Agent Reno asked. "Relatives or friends?"

"Kim's mother is in Oregon and her father is dead," Ryker said. "She never mentioned siblings and I don't know her friends." He tried to rein in his frustration that law enforcement had been so close to apprehending Mick and Kim but hadn't been able to get to them in time. "I haven't seen Kim in three years. And I never knew Mick well. I met him exactly once, when he came to help my wife move out of our home. We didn't have much to say to each other." Only later had he run Mick's name through the police department database and seen his rap sheet. Knowing Kim had chosen a man like that over him had been one more knife to the gut.

"And you're absolutely sure you had no idea this was coming?" Agent Cussler asked. "Your wife hadn't made threats to you, or talked about regaining custody of your daughter?" Cussler sounded as if he couldn't believe this was even possible.

"I had not heard one word from my *ex-wife* in three years," Ryker said, struggling to keep his voice even. "Neither had Charlotte."

"So your ex-wife hadn't called or written to your daughter, maybe without your knowing?" Cussler continued.

"Charlotte is four," Ryker said. "She can't read yet, and she doesn't have a phone."

"The preschool said they never heard from Ms. Vernon," Agent Reno said. "They never saw anyone matching her description near the day care, either."

"We have a witness who saw a woman she believes was Kim Vernon at a local bar the night before Charlotte disappeared," Travis said.

"Yes, we read your report," Cussler said. "Are you sure of this witness's identification?"

"The description she gave sounded like Kim to me," Ryker said.

"People sometimes give reports like this in order to insert themselves into a case and gain a little of the spotlight," Cussler said.

"I know this woman and she's not like that," Ryker said. Or, he had known Harper once. She couldn't have changed that much.

Cussler nodded and made a check mark in his notebook. Did he have an actual to-do list in there?

"Are you sure about the identification from the witness in Utah?" Ryker asked.

"The description the man gave fit the one broadcast for your daughter, your ex-wife and her paramour," Cussler said. "Why? Do you think they wouldn't go to Utah?"

Ryker tried to recall if he had ever heard anyone use the word *paramour* before, then forced himself to address the question. He might not like Agent Cussler, but the man had a job to do and Ryker needed to help him do it. "They might go to Utah," he conceded. He glanced at the sheriff. "Kim said she and Mick wanted to move somewhere away from people and live off the land."

"There are people who come to Utah looking for a place like that," Reno said.

Ryker nodded. "But people try to do that here, too. You can still buy mining claims cheap. Or maybe they decided to just squat on a piece of land they thought was vacant and scrounge for what they needed to build a place."

"We've recently had an uptick in vandalism in the high country," Travis said. "Someone has been stealing building materials."

Ryker swiveled toward him. "Mick strikes me as the type who would think he shouldn't have to pay for building materials if people were careless enough to just leave them lying around. And maybe once they got here, and Kim realized how close she was to Charlotte, she decided to just…take her."

"An impulsive move," Travis said.

"Right. Because Kim was impulsive. She never liked to wait for anything she wanted."

Agents Cussler and Reno shook their heads. "It doesn't make sense for them to kidnap a child and then stay here," Cussler said.

"If they are here, why not just drive up there and arrest them?" Reno asked.

"Because there are thousands of acres of unoccupied wilderness in this county alone," Ryker said.

"There are a lot of places to hide," Travis added.

"Utah makes more sense." Cussler closed his notebook. "We'll be in touch if we have any more information."

Travis escorted the agents from the room, but he returned a few minutes later. "Do you really think your ex and her boyfriend are up there on some abandoned mining claim?" Travis asked.

"I don't know. It just…feels right." He forced himself to

meet the sheriff's gaze. Travis had a reputation as a hard man, but all Ryker saw now was compassion. "I need to look for them," he said. "I'll take time off work to do it, if you want."

"You don't have to take time off," Travis said. "And we'll look with you. We know this county better than the feds, anyway. But I wasn't exaggerating when I said there are a lot of places to hide. It could take a while to find them."

Ryker stood, feeling stronger than he had in the last twenty-four hours. "I'll spend as long as it takes."

Chapter Five

"Harper, I have a new project I want you and Devlin to work on." Patterson approached Harper's drawing table, a sheaf of rolled papers in his hand. In his forties, Patterson kept his head shaved smooth and wore his usual uniform of jeans and a denim shirt with the sleeves rolled up. She suspected he had a closet full of the exact same shirt. Devlin moved in beside them as Patterson unrolled the papers and began pinning them to the table's surface. Today Devlin sported black trousers, a white short-sleeved shirt, suspenders and a string tie. Harper, whose approach to getting ready for work was to pull the first thing from her closet—today it was a navy sheath dress and flats—wondered how either of the men had arrived at their sense of style. Would it be liberating or confining to be so committed to a single way of dressing?

"This resort development in California wants us to update their maps," Patterson said. "There are five sections." He indicated the five 11-by-14-inch sheets tacked to the work table. "The place has been around since the 1980s. These maps were done in 2000, but obviously, there's been lots of changes. They're sending files with aerial views of the entire place which I need you two to incorporate into updated maps of each section. They want something artistic, in keeping with their current style. You'll get a feel for that on their website. They want to frame the maps in their office and common areas and have smaller versions to hand out to interested members, visitors and potential buyers."

"Looks like fun," Devlin said. He leaned over the drawing table and squinted at one of the maps. "Looks like they've got stables and riding trails, and a golf course." He grinned at Harper. "Think we could talk them into comping us a visit? Strictly for research purposes, of course."

Harper returned the smile. Though visiting a resort by herself—or even with Dev for company—didn't sound as much fun as going with a romantic partner.

With Ryker.

She pushed the thought away. She was sure the last thing on Ryker's mind right now was romance. "Has anyone heard anything more about the search for Charlotte Vernon?" she asked.

"I haven't," Patterson said.

Devlin shook his head. "That poor kid. And poor dad." He began untacking two of the maps. "I'll start matching these up with the aerial photos. You take two others and we'll work on the fifth together when these are done."

"Sounds good." She moved to her computer and downloaded the aerial files, then searched for the resort website. But she couldn't focus on the photos of smiling couples on the golf course and trails, and the upbeat prose about the benefits of life with every amenity right outside the front door. Her thoughts continually shifted to Charlotte and Ryker. Where was that dear child, and how was Ryker enduring the torture of not knowing?

"Harper?"

The familiar, low voice made her jump and she looked up to see Ryker himself, in his sheriff's department uniform, walking toward her desk. "Ryker, how are you?" She rose and started to give him a hug, then thought better of it, aware of Devlin and her other coworkers in the open-plan office watching.

Ryker looked around the space, which featured large windows on three sides and drawing tables and desks, as well as long counters for spreading out large-format pieces scattered throughout. Everything was white and pale blue and filled with light. Finally, his gaze came to rest on her once more. He looked tired, but determined. "I need your help," he said.

"Anything."

"Someone at the county clerk's office told me this office has maps of all the mining claims in the high country. She said you actually drew the maps the county has, and can produce them in a larger format than she had available, with more detail."

"Yes, we do." She moved to the far corner of the room, to the large, flat file drawers that held copies of all the work they had done. "If we don't have what you need here, we can print them for you."

He came to stand beside her, close enough that she could hear the clink of the various implements on his duty belt each time he moved, and the low hiss of static from his shoulder-mounted radio. "What exactly are you looking for?" she asked.

"Mining claims above ten-thousand-feet elevation," he said. "Above that point, county building codes don't allow for permanent residences, but people buy the places to camp in the summer or because they want to reopen the mines."

"Are you thinking they would be good places to hide?" she asked.

He moved closer and lowered his voice. "I think Kim and her boyfriend might be camping or in some kind of makeshift shelter on one of those claims. When we split up, she talked about wanting to live somewhere off-grid and said when she did she would take Charlotte to live with her. I used to worry she was serious, and I told her she would never get custody. Maybe that was a mistake. Rather than go through legal channels, I believe she decided to just take Charlotte."

Harper studied the labels on the drawers, then opened one. "The maps are organized by mining districts," she said. "We don't have information about who owns each claim. You'd have to get that from the county."

"Do you have topographical maps?" he asked. "I'm trying to get an idea of the terrain."

"We can do better than that," she said. "On our computers, we'll have the aerial photographs and even satellite imagery we used to compile the maps."

"That's exactly what I need."

She pulled out half a dozen large maps, then led him into a separate workroom with a long table and a fifty-inch monitor. "It's going to take me a minute to find the photographs," she said. "But you can study the maps while I'm looking." While she waited for the computer to boot up, she swiveled her chair to watch him. He bent over the table, studying one of the unrolled maps. "How are you going to narrow down where to look for them?" she asked.

"I'll start by looking for places accessible by roads. Mick has a Jeep registered in his name. Anything with a structure on it would be good. There are a lot of those claims that have been abandoned and ownership has gone back to the county because of unpaid taxes. If I was going to squat on a property, I would choose one of those."

"Maybe they bought one of the claims," she said.

"I checked with the county and there's no record of that. Since neither of them have held any kind of regular job for the past three years that I can determine, I don't think that's likely."

"How do they support themselves?" she asked.

"They work off the books. Odd jobs. Mick has been convicted twice of fraud, so maybe he's got a new swindle police haven't learned about yet. And there's old-fashioned theft. He's been convicted of that, too."

She turned back to the computer. "Kim was a law-abiding citizen when I met her," he said, as if he had read her thoughts. "I guess she was looking for someone who was my exact opposite when she got together with Mick."

"Your marriage lasted longer than mine," she said as she began to scroll through the list of photographic files. "Franco and I only made it thirteen months, but we managed to part as friends."

"Oh." So much emotion behind that one word. "I didn't know you'd been married."

She shrugged. "I was lonely. I thought getting married would fix that, but I was wrong."

"Yeah. I was lonely when I met Kim, too."

"At least you ended up with Charlotte."

"I would have been reasonable, open to some kind of visitation arrangement, but that wasn't good enough for Kim and Mick. Now she's going to find out how unreasonable I can be."

She smiled in spite of herself. That was the Ryker she had fallen so hard for when she was seventeen. He had been full of righteous anger and tough-guy swagger, with a black leather jacket, a motorcycle and an attitude. And tender as a marshmallow inside, though most people didn't get to see that side. They had judged him so harshly when Aiden was taken. She had believed they were wrong, but her parents had whisked her away before she had the chance to tell him.

"What do you have for me to look at?" He was back to business. Maybe now wasn't the time to bring up that old hurt.

"I have the set of aerial photos pulled up that corresponds to the Galloway Basin district," she said. "You're welcome to look at them here, but I can also load them and the others onto a flash drive for you to review at the sheriff's department."

"I'd like the files to take with me, but I'd also like to study them here," he said. "We don't have a monitor like this available at the sheriff's department."

"You're welcome to do that." She brought up the first photo, an aerial view showing a narrow dirt road running alongside a section of land with few trees, and a half-collapsed structure of rusting metal and silvery wood. "You can zoom in, scan out, and even highlight a section to print if you like," she said, demonstrating these functions. "Let me know if you need anything."

She slid out of the chair and he took her place, already focused on the screen.

"Can I get you some coffee?" she asked.

"What? Oh, no thanks."

She stood behind him for a moment, watching as he guided the cursor across the photo, zooming in on the ruins, then backing out and switching to the next photograph. What, exactly, was he looking for? Was there any way she could help him?

If he wanted more help, he would ask, she told herself. And she had work to do.

She left the room quietly and returned to her desk. Devlin looked up from his computer. "Everything okay?"

"He's looking at maps that might help with the search for his daughter."

Three hours later, she was debating suggesting Ryker take a break for lunch when he emerged from the back room. "Did you find anything useful?" she asked.

"I think so." He stopped beside her desk. "Thanks."

"If there's anything I can do to help, just ask," she said. "I could help with the search. Everyone here would."

He shook his head. "We can't risk civilians running around those old mines. Though if we narrow the search area, we might call on search and rescue."

"If that happens, I'll be there." She looked down at her desk, suddenly feeling awkward. "And if you ever just want to talk, I'm here for that, too."

"Thanks." He covered her hand with his, and she felt the shock of that contact, and looked into his eyes. She saw the same awareness there—a connection she had thought long-severed flickering to life. Then he pulled his hand away. "I'd better go."

"Poor guy," Devlin said after the door shut behind Ryker. "Being a cop he's probably tortured by all the horrible things that might have happened to his daughter."

She wanted to tell him that Charlotte was going to be all right, that she'd been kidnapped by her mother. But she didn't know anything about Kim or her boyfriend, did she? Maybe Charlotte wouldn't be all right with them. The thought made her sick. She wanted to do something to help, to comfort Ryker and his family. But she wasn't really part of his life anymore.

BACK AT THE sheriff's department, Ryker showed Travis and Declan the maps and aerial photography he had collected. He unrolled one of the maps on the table in the conference room and the three men bent over it. "We could start by comparing what's in these photos to existing structures,"

Ryker said. "We can drive up and take a closer look at any new or altered structures."

"Best to do that from the air," Declan said. "Maybe we can find someone to fly us over. We might even be able to hitch a ride in a fire-spotter plane. They're making regular patrols in the area this time of year."

"I think that would be safer than approaching on foot or even in a department vehicle," Travis said. "Declan, make some calls and see what you can arrange. In the meantime, have you seen this?"

He slipped a folded newspaper from beneath his arm and offered it to Ryker. Ryker opened the paper and stared at the article filling the bottom of the page:

Search for Missing Girl Focuses on Utah

The search for missing toddler Charlotte Vernon, who disappeared from her day care in the western mountain community of Eagle Mountain on Wednesday, is now focused in Utah, after what FBI officials have termed a credible sighting of the little girl with a couple at a campground outside Moab on Thursday.

The woman the child was seen with matches the description of her estranged mother, twenty-nine-year-old Kimberley "Kim" Vernon, who is suspected of kidnapping the child. Since her divorce from Charlotte's father, Rayford County sheriff's deputy Ryker Vernon three years ago, Ms. Vernon has reportedly had no contact with her daughter. Mr. Ryker was awarded sole custody of the child as part of the divorce proceedings.

Mother and daughter are alleged to be in the company of Michael "Mick" Davis, described as a thirty-five-year-old drifter with a criminal record for theft, assault, fraud and a number of other offenses. If you see the trio, do not attempt to approach, but contact law enforcement immediately.

The article was accompanied by photos of Charlotte, Kim and Mick. Mick's picture was clearly a mug shot. Ryker didn't know where Kim's photo had come from, though it looked as if it had been enlarged from a snapshot, one taken outdoors in the summer, Kim squinting into the camera, a breeze pushing her hair to one side.

Charlotte's image was the recent school photo Ryker had provided that was printed on posters all over the county. Her big smile showed off a row of pearly baby teeth and the deep dimples on either side of her mouth. Her blue eyes shone with excitement. He laid the paper aside. "Have there been any more sightings?" he asked.

"Not that we've heard," Travis said. "Not here or in Utah."

"I could be wrong about them still being here," Ryker said. "I could be wasting our time, but I don't think so." He stared at the map showing the winding mountain roads, timber-framed adits and weathered ruins of the Galloway Basin mining district. "This is something I think Kim would do."

"Fleeing to Utah would make it harder for you to find her," Declan said.

"I don't think she would see it that way." He hesitated, trying to find the words to explain the puzzling woman he had married. "She liked to taunt people. She believed she was better than anyone else—that her ideas, or Mick's ideas that she adopted, were better. She's probably convinced herself that whatever she had planned for this off-grid lifestyle is so superior to the way everyone else is living that

Charlotte will naturally want to stay with her, whether I ever find her or not."

"What about Mick?" Travis asked. "Any insight into how he thinks?"

Ryker shook his head. "I don't know much more about him than you do. I've studied his criminal record. As a felon, he's not supposed to own firearms, but he probably does. Kim probably bought them for him. Or he stole them. She said living off-grid was his idea, but she was all for it."

"Having a base of operations near but out of reach of a lot of people in a generally well-off town like Eagle Mountain might be tempting," Declan said. "Lots of summer homes and vacation properties to rob when they're unoccupied. Lots of tourists to rip off. A relatively small sheriff's department Davis probably believes he can outwit."

"It's worth looking into more closely," Travis said. He nodded to the maps. "Give us some places to focus on. Declan, see about that plane. I'll get in touch with the FBI and see if they have anything else to tell us."

When he was alone in the room, Ryker bent over the maps. Given free rein, his mind would have focused on Charlotte. Was she afraid? Tired and dirty? Hungry? Did she miss him?

He didn't have the luxury of indulging in such thoughts. The only way to get through this was to keep moving forward. To do whatever he could to find his daughter. He pulled out a notebook and pen and focused on the maps. He needed to come up with a plan.

Chapter Six

Friday afternoon, Harper's mother called and invited her to dinner, so Harper headed there after work. Her parents' two-story, cedar-sided home was in a neighborhood of similar homes built in the mid-to-late-1990s, showing its age but still well-cared for. Harper parked in the driveway in front of the garage and—as she always did when she visited— looked up to the right front bedroom, which had been hers for most of her life. She had last checked the bedroom about ten days ago, and it had been exactly as she left it, as if her parents were expecting her to move back in any moment.

She knocked, then let herself in the front door. "I'm in the kitchen!" her mother shouted. Harper headed in that direction, but stopped in the living room to say hello to her father, who was watching a World War II documentary on television. Tom Stanick was a self-employed financial advisor. For as long as Harper could remember, he had rented an office above the local bank. Time had added silver to his still-thick hair, and more lines around his eyes and mouth, but he was still a handsome man. "Hello, sweetie," he said. "What a nice surprise."

"Mom called and invited me to dinner."

"That's nice, but you know you don't have to wait for an invitation. You can stop by anytime."

"I know, Dad." He, especially, seemed to miss having her in the house. She was an only child, which meant they had no one else to focus on. It had taken her a long time to forgive them after the way they had acted over her pregnancy, but her ire had gradually faded. They had wanted the best for her, and after her miscarriage they had been gentle with her, welcoming her back home and encouraging her to think of the future and her education.

Ryker was gone by the time she'd returned to Eagle Mountain, and she didn't stay long either, moving that fall to Ohio, where she had enrolled in a small arts college and pursued a degree in graphic arts.

Tension between her and her mother had increased after she had eloped with Franco, a Bronx-born musician who her mother, especially, hadn't approved of. But Valerie had gritted her teeth and tried to be welcoming. "I'm sure we'll feel more comfortable with him once we know him better," she had said after meeting him for the first time at their wedding.

But he and Harper had been together such a short time that a second meeting had never happened.

Harper had been determined to build a new life on her own in Ohio after the divorce, but the company she worked for folded and she had been unable to find a new job. When her dad contacted her about an opening at Taylor Geographic, she had resisted the idea. But of course, the job was perfect, and her parents had welcomed her back with open arms. She had lived with them for six weeks before finding her own apartment in Eagle Mountain, but in that time they had settled into a new peace. She was ready to move on with her life, and that meant letting go of her resentment over how things had worked out with Ryker, and their role in that.

"Hi, Mom." Harper hugged her mom around the shoulders, and snatched a piece of carrot she was chopping for salad.

"Hello, Harper. You can set the table. Dinner is almost ready."

While Harper set the table, her dad came in and filled water glasses, so that when her mother carried the steaming platter of spaghetti and meatballs to the table, all was ready. This was how so many evenings in her life had started— the three of them gathered at this same oak table, chatting about their day or the latest happenings in town. The very sameness of these moments over the years comforted her. She hoped one day she would have a family that could build this kind of tradition.

"I just saw a news bulletin about that missing child," her dad said as he scooped salad onto his plate. "They think the couple suspected of taking her are driving a white Jeep."

"Well, I hope they find her soon," her mom said. "You can't go anywhere without seeing that poor child's face on a poster."

"Apparently, they suspect Ryker's ex-wife of kidnapping her and taking her to Utah," her dad said.

Her mom shook a bottle of salad dressing. "I don't know how a man like Ryker ended up with sole custody of a little girl," she said.

Harper tried to let a lot of things her mother said to annoy her slide, but this wasn't going to be one of them. "Ryker is a wonderful father and he's sick about Charlotte being gone," she said. "And the reason he ended up with sole custody is because her mother abandoned her."

Her mom froze and fixed her daughter with a gaze sharper than the knife she was using to slice into a meatball. "How do you know this?" she demanded. "Have you talked to him?"

"Yes, I've talked to him. Ryker is my friend, and he's going through something terrible right now."

The meatball was too tender to require the ferocity with which her mother was attacking it. "I don't like the idea of you seeing him again," she said.

"This isn't about what you like, Mother." Harper forced herself to pause and breathe deeply. She wasn't a sullen teenager anymore. They could discuss this like adults. "And I'm not seeing him. He came by the office today to get some maps. For the sheriff's department."

"Ryker has done well for himself, getting that job as a sheriff's deputy," her dad said.

Harper sent her father a grateful smile, but she didn't keep the expression long, as her mother said, "I'm surprised he was able to become a law enforcement officer, considering his past."

"He didn't do anything wrong." Harper laid down her fork, her appetite vanished. "He was cleared of all charges."

Her mother looked away. "I'm entitled to my opinion. And you can't say Ryker was good to you. As soon as you were out of sight, he left town and ended up married to an awful woman who has now kidnapped his child."

"You kept us apart," Harper said. "He probably thinks I left him. And he certainly had no idea his ex-wife would kidnap Charlotte. That's a terrible thing to say."

"I stand by my opinion."

Her father sent Harper a look that told her not to waste her time arguing with her mother. She focused on her food, though she scarcely tasted the meal as she ate. This wasn't a new conversation for them, but her mother's refusal to see Ryker in any other light frustrated her almost beyond bearing.

When dinner was over, she thanked her mom and prepared to leave, but her father said, "Harper and I will do the dishes, dear."

"Thanks for not arguing with your mother," her dad said when he and Harper were scraping plates and loading the dishwasher. "I know it's not always easy."

"Why is she so set against Ryker? He didn't do anything wrong."

"I'm not trying to justify her feelings, but losing a child is every parent's worst nightmare. When Aiden disappeared, your mother was so upset. And when they accused Ryker of being involved, all she could see was that her only child was in danger. She can't let go of that feeling."

Harper slid a handful of silverware into the basket on the door of the machine. "It's ridiculous. The Vernons are very nice and Ryker is a good man. And from what I've seen, he's a great father, and he's worried sick about Charlotte."

"You're not a teenager anymore. You get to decide who you want as a friend. And for what it's worth, I don't think Ryker would be a bad choice."

"Thanks, Dad. That means a lot."

"Your mother loves you and she doesn't want to see you hurt, but that doesn't mean she's right about everything."

There were plenty of days when Harper thought she herself might be wrong about everything. Acknowledging that made it a little easier to forgive others' mistaken opinions. She had certainly thought she had been wrong about Ryker in those lonely days after her miscarriage, when he never responded to the letter she had written, giving him the news. But in her heart, she had never believed he would be so cold. When he told her he never received her letter, she felt the truth of his words, and that particular wound, at least, was less painful.

"Search and rescue may go to search for Charlotte again soon," she said.

"Good luck. And be careful."

"I always am." At least with her physical body. With her heart…maybe not so much.

STRAPPED INTO THE passenger seat in the cockpit of the small fixed-wing aircraft—which was parked at the airfield in Delta—on Saturday morning, Ryker tried to pay attention to the safety briefing the pilot was giving him. Alissa Mayfield had short, sandy hair and freckles and said she had been flying planes for twenty years. Ryker studied the array of dials, gauges, switches and lights in front of her and thought brain surgery might be easier than sorting out all of that. Alissa followed his gaze and laughed. "It's not as complicated as it looks," she said. "Trust me, I know what I'm doing." She handed him a headset. "It gets really noisy in the air. This will protect your ears, and there's a speaker and microphone so we can communicate."

He donned the headset and heard her voice in his ear. "You want to take a look at Galloway Basin and the Camp Frederick area, is that right?" she asked.

"Right. I want to look at the undeveloped mining claims in the area for any signs of new or updated construction. And any vehicles parked on any of the claims." Or a little girl who might run out to wave at a plane. If that happened, it was going to take everything in him not to insist they land immediately.

"Got it. I can fly pretty low with this in most areas, but let me know if there's anything you want to take a better look at." The engine started and the roar—even muffled by the headset—vibrated through him.

The plane taxied down the runway and he gripped the

seat. He wasn't a fan of heights when he was standing still, but this sensation of rushing down the runway, then rising into the air made his palms sweat and his breath come in gasps.

But then they were soaring, the ground falling away quickly. "It's a good day for flying," Alissa said. "Nice and calm."

He couldn't help but think of the aerial photography he had been poring over the previous day. They followed the silver ribbon of the highway over Dixon Pass for a while, then angled west, soaring over dense stands of fir and spruce, the roofs of luxury homes set among the trees. Then the trees grew less prominent, and the landscape was dominated by rock in sunset shades from yellow and orange to a red so deep it was almost purple. "This is the Galloway Basin area," she said. "I think most of the mining claims you're looking at are above tree line."

"That's right." Forgetting his fear of heights, he leaned forward to peer out the side window, past the wing of the plane to the scenery below. He was reminded of the train sets he had seen set up in museums. There were no trains here, only the scars of dirt roads winding among old tree stumps that were once evergreens cut for their timber for the mines over a century ago. Colorful spills of mine waste flowed like melted candle wax down the sides of the mountains, and piles of gray rock marked the openings where trams had once been loaded with ore to be transported to stamp mills. The rusted, bent tram rails stitched across the landscape in places, along with snarls of cables from the old overhead trams. Clusters of gray lumber were all that remained of the buildings that had once housed hundreds of miners and support staff, while isolated cabins marked the smaller claims, where one or two people had tried to wrest riches from the mountains.

They flew over an expanse of treeless green—startling in its emerald lushness—through patches of orangey-brown, like stains on velvet, that marked clumps of beetle-killed timber. "That's the old Alexander mine." Alissa pointed to their right. "Those grass berms and holding ponds are part of the mitigation process to leach the arsenic, magnesium and other hazardous metals from the water before it empties into the river or soaks into the soil."

They flew on. Ryker spotted a cow moose and her calf, a trio of backpack-laden hikers climbing up a trail leading to the top of a peak, and clusters of Jeeps on the backroads like the toy cars he had played with on the living room rug as a boy. But no one who looked out of place. And no sign of life on any of the claims.

"We need to head back now," Alissa said after a while.

"Okay," he answered.

He was too distracted by thoughts of Charlotte to even be nervous about the landing. When they were on the ground and the plane was silent, they removed their headsets and he unbuckled his seat belt. "Thanks for taking me up," he said.

"I'll go out with you again, whenever you want," she said. "I've got two kids of my own."

"Thanks. I may take you up on that."

He returned to the sheriff's department to pore over more maps and photographs, hoping to spot some clue that would lead him to the right place. The alternative was to go home and do nothing, and he couldn't bear that. But all these mining claims were beginning to look alike, and there were a lot of trees obscuring some claims. It would be so easy to overlook the very place Kim and Mick were hiding.

The door opened and Gage stood there. "I thought I saw

the light on," he said. "You look like you've been here a while."

"What time is it?" Ryker stretched, his neck popping loudly as he did so.

"After seven." Gage moved into the room. "I heard you went up in a plane today."

"I did. But I didn't see anything."

"There's a lot of territory to cover."

"Yeah. And maybe the feds are right and they're in Utah."

Gage rested one hip in the table and crossed his arms. "Four years ago, my little girl Casey disappeared," he said. "She wasn't kidnapped, she was lost, up on Dakota Ridge."

"I didn't know that. How long was she missing?"

"Three days, but it seemed like a lot longer. She wasn't my daughter then, I was just a deputy on the scene, but I was still worried sick. My wife, Maya, was Casey's aunt. Casey's parents—Maya's brother and his wife—were murdered. Casey got away and was hiding in the woods, afraid to come out. She was only five, and she's hard of hearing. The search for her is how I met Maya. We ended up adopting Casey. Anyway, that's all to say I know a little of what you're going through and I hope you have the same good outcome."

"How's Casey doing?"

"She had nightmares for a while. And sometimes she misses her parents. But overall, she's doing good." He smiled. "She's crazy about the baby, so that's good. I hope they'll be close."

"Thanks for telling me."

"Yeah, well, what you're going through has me and Maya reliving all of that."

He nodded. "I keep thinking about my cousin, Aiden."

"I remember when that happened," Gage said.

"People thought I was responsible."

"But you weren't."

"No. But they never found his killer. Some people still aren't convinced of my innocence."

"You can't worry about them." He stood. "Focus on the people who are supporting you. Anything you need at all, just ask."

"Thanks." But what he needed was his daughter. Kim was the only person who could give her back and right now that wasn't happening.

Seven years ago

"You have the right to remain silent. Anything you say can and will be used against you in a court of law."

"But I haven't done anything wrong," Ryker interrupted the beefy, blond sheriff's deputy who stood in front of him.

"You have the right to an attorney…" The deputy droned on with the rest of the warning Ryker had only heard previously on TV shows. He didn't look up from the card in his hand until he had read it all. "Do you understand what I just read you?" he asked.

"Yes," Ryker said. "Yes, sir."

"Sit down." The deputy indicated a wooden, straight-backed chair in the small, brightly lit room. "We have some questions for you."

"You said I didn't have to say anything," Ryker said.

"That's right." The deputy—his name tag said Rollins—crossed his arms over his barrel chest. He had thinning blond hair, the pink scalp showing through at the back. "But if you didn't do anything wrong cooperating with us will have you out of here sooner rather than later."

"Okay." He definitely wanted out of here. The deputy

had driven him away from his cousin's house before his parents arrived. Did they even know where he was?

"Tell us what happened with the little boy, Aiden."

Ryker related the same story he had told multiple times by now—how he had put Aiden to bed at eight, fallen asleep while watching TV, checked on the boy about nine and found the window open, the screen off and the boy gone.

"So you're saying someone removed the screen, climbed in that window and took the little boy out of bed while you were in the next room and you never heard a thing?" Deputy Rollins squinted as if trying to make out something in the distance.

"Yes, sir. And I wasn't in the next room, I was down the hall." Still, why hadn't he heard anything? Surely, Aiden would have cried out.

"I find that hard to believe." Rollins leaned across the table toward him. "What I believe is that maybe the little boy was fussy, giving you a hard time. Maybe you lost your temper and hit him. An accident. Maybe he fell and hit his head and wouldn't wake up. It scared you, so you decided to hide the body and fake a kidnapping."

Ryker stared. "No! Aiden's a good kid. And he's just a kid. I'd never hurt him."

Rollins slammed his fist down on the table, making Ryker jump. "You need to tell us the truth, so we can find the boy. His poor parents are wrecks, wondering what happened to him. You're the only one who can help them."

"I don't know where he is," Ryker said. "You need to find him."

"You listen to me, kid." Rollins put his face so close to Ryker's he could smell onions on his breath. "I know nobody took that boy but you. You need to tell the truth."

A loud knock sounded on the door. Rollins looked up. "Who is it?"

"Carson Shay. I'm Mr. Vernon's attorney."

Ryker thought for a moment that Rollins wasn't going to answer, but after a moment, he straightened and went to the door. "Vernon hasn't asked for an attorney," he said.

"His father called me." He looked past Rollins to Ryker. "Hello, son. How are you doing?"

Not so good, Ryker thought. "I'm glad to see you," he said.

"Mr. Vernon won't be answering any more questions tonight," Shay said. He moved past the cop into the room. Rollins glared at them both, then left them alone. After the door shut, Ryker clenched his hands into fists, trying to stop himself from shaking.

"I didn't do anything wrong," he said. "I don't know where Aiden is. Why aren't they looking for him?"

"There are people looking." Shay stood in the same place Rollins had stood. He was probably in his late-thirties, with black, curly hair and black-rimmed glasses. He wore khakis and a dress shirt, but no tie, and was freshly shaven, even though it had to be after eleven at night. "I know you've probably gone over this a lot already, but I need you to tell me again what happened."

So once again, Ryker told his story and relived the horror of finding Aiden's bed empty and the window open. Shay made notes and nodded. When Ryker fell silent, Shay said, "They don't have enough evidence to charge you, so I'm going to take you home. But they will probably question you again. Tell them you won't talk without your attorney present. Then call me."

"Why do they think I did it?"

"You were right there in front of them. They came up with a story they thought fit. It's a lazy approach, but it happens. They'll try to find evidence to fit their story. My job is to hold their feet to the fire and insist they look at everything, not just the parts that make their job easy." He clapped his hand on Ryker's shoulder. "Let's get you home."

"Do other people think I hurt Aiden?" Ryker asked.

The fine lines around Shay's eyes deepened. "Some people will. You'll find out who your real friends are."

Harper, Ryker thought. *I have to talk to Harper.* "What time is it?" he asked.

Shay checked his watch. "It's ten minutes to one."

He couldn't call Harper now. She'd be asleep. He would call her tomorrow. She was going to have his baby. She needed to know he was innocent.

Except when he did finally call her, she was already gone.

Chapter Seven

Harper was sleeping in on Sunday when her text alert sounded. Groggy, she groped for the phone on her bedside table and squinted at the message. One man and dog fallen down mine shaft, Ida B Mine, off Stoney Gulch Jeep trail.

Fully awake now, she sat up and texted that she was on her way. Ten minutes later, she was dressed and headed out the door. She gathered with seven other volunteers at search and rescue headquarters. Ryan and Eldon were out of town on a climbing trip, Hannah and Jake were both working, and several other volunteers were unavailable for one reason or another. That left Danny, Tony, Caleb, Christine, Sheri, Carrie and Harper to load gear into the rescue vehicle and head into the mountains.

"I don't think I've ever been to the Ida B Mine," Harper said as Caleb guided the specially outfitted Jeep up a steep and rocky trail scarcely wide enough for the vehicle.

"There's not much up there," Christine said. "But it's near enough the trail into Crystal Basin that some people detour to poke around among the ruins."

"And apparently, fall down mine shafts," Danny said.

Half a mile farther on, a woman waved them down. She wore a red fleece top and gray hiking pants, her dark hair in a long braid down her back. "I'm the one who called in the emergency," she said. "My boyfriend and my dog are stuck down in this mine shaft."

"How much farther can we drive?" Caleb asked.

"Maybe another hundred yards? There's kind of a flat spot at the end of the road where you can park."

They proceeded slowly, the woman, Rachel, walking alongside them. From her they learned that the man and the dog—a golden retriever—were mostly unhurt, but the man might have sprained his ankle. Neither of them were able to climb out of the shaft, which was about a hundred feet deep. Caleb parked on a level gravel strip at the end of the road and Danny and Sheri hiked ahead with Rachel, while the others unloaded anything they thought they might need for the retrieval, including ropes, helmets, first aid gear and a special harness designed for dogs.

By the time they were finished, Danny and Sheri returned. "The guy's name is Scott," Danny said. "Twenty-something, in good physical shape, no medications or health conditions. His dog, Ginger, was chasing a pika in some rock rubble and suddenly disappeared. Scott could hear her barking and went in search of her. He found her at the bottom of the shaft and thought he could get to her and bring her back up, but it was a lot farther than he estimated and he ended up slipping and falling and hurting his ankle. He says he doesn't think it's broken, but it's swollen and he can't put much weight on it. The dog is fine, but they're both stuck down there. Luckily his girlfriend, Rachel, was able to get a phone signal and call for help. She even tossed a pack with some water and snacks down to him so he's been fine, just ready to get out of there."

"So this shaft opening was hidden by the rocks?" Caleb asked.

"Yeah, you can't see it until you're right up on it," Danny

said. "We flagged it with a stick and a red bandana so none of us accidentally fall in."

"I thought there was a law that open shafts had to be covered," Christina said.

"There's some concrete and iron strapping around this one, like it might have been covered at one time, but that's gone now," Sheri said. She picked up a coil of rope. "I'm going to go down in the shaft and get the dog in the harness to haul up, then I'll send the guy up and we'll see to his foot. It looks like there's only room for one person at a time down there."

She led the way back to the shaft. The others followed, each carrying gear. Harper carried the dog sling and a safety helmet. By the time she reached the group around the shaft, Tony and Caleb where already setting anchors and arranging ropes to allow them to haul Scott and Ginger to the surface. Rachel sat cross-legged beside the shaft, relaying instructions to Scott. Occasionally, the dog barked.

Harper listened to Tony's instructions about setting the ropes, then stood back while Sheri, wearing a safety helmet, harness, and a pack, climbed down into the shaft. The dog's barking increased, amplified by the rocky sides of the shaft.

Less than ten minutes later, Tony and Danny began hauling on the ropes. They had fashioned a pulley over the center of the shaft in order to raise the dog without scraping her against the shaft walls. She rose into the air, looking confused, but remaining still until she spotted Rachel, then she began wagging her tail wildly. She greeted her rescuers with enthusiastic whimpers and wet kisses as they unfastened the harness. "Let me get the leash on her before you let her go," Rachel said. "I don't want her falling back down there."

Raising Scott took longer, and required the strength of

Tony, Danny and Caleb, but he also rode a sling to the top. He was able to sit on the side of the shaft and swing his legs over until he was clear of the opening. While he was still in the harness and wearing the helmet, Danny, a registered nurse, tended to his swollen ankle.

Sheri emerged shortly after, quickly scaling the shaft with little assistance. Scott insisted he could walk to the search and rescue vehicle with a little support, so with Caleb on one side and Tony on the other, he started down the trail, Rachel and Ginger right behind them.

The others began gathering the rope and other scattered equipment. One of the helmets rolled down an incline and Harper ran to retrieve it, almost tripping over a piece of rusty metal as she did so. She stopped to examine it. "Hey!" she called to the others. "Come look at this."

Christine was the first to respond to her cry, followed by Carrie and Sheri. "What is it?" Sheri asked.

"I think it's the cover that's supposed to be on top of that shaft." Harper bent and tugged at the metal strap fastened to the edge of a square iron grate.

Christine and Sheri helped her drag the heavy grate from the rocks that half-covered it. Harper studied the edges of the strapping. "This didn't rust away," she said. "Someone deliberately cut it."

"Why would they do that?" Christine asked.

"Maybe they thought there was gold in the mine and wanted to get down in it?" Carrie suggested.

"It hasn't been here that long," Sheri said. "There's not much dirt on it, and no plants growing up through it. It's almost like someone tried to hide it under the rocks."

"Let's drag it back over the opening so no one else falls in," Harper said.

The women managed to lift the heavy grate and walk it

over to the shaft, where they positioned it over the opening. It fit perfectly. They piled rocks around the edges to further secure it.

Harper walked back over to where the grate had been hidden. "What are you looking for?" Christine called.

"I don't know," she admitted. "I'm just trying to figure out why someone would do that." A flash of bright pink in the rocks a few feet away drew her attention and she picked her way toward it. At first, she thought it was surveyor's tape, the kind used to mark property boundaries. Maybe it had originally been tied to the grate to make it more visible. But when she knelt and pulled the pink strip from the rocks, she was startled to find herself holding a length of satin ribbon.

"What have you got?" Christine asked, coming up behind her.

Harper stared at the ribbon, stomach churning. "It's a ribbon," she said. "A little girl's hair ribbon."

"THAT'S CHARLOTTE'S HAIR RIBBON, I'm sure of it." Ryker stared at the once-bright pink ribbon, now dirty and frayed. Half an inch wide and about a foot long, the ribbon still bore the creases from where it had been tied into a bow. He remembered watching his mother make that bow one morning earlier that week. He looked up at Harper, who had walked into the sheriff's department three minutes before, ribbon in hand. "Where, exactly, did you find it?"

"At the Ida B Mine, off Stoney Gulch Road. Search and rescue were called up there this morning to retrieve a man and a dog from a mine shaft they had fallen into." She glanced over at Travis and Gage Walker, who stood to her left, both in identical postures, arms crossed over their chests. "Someone had removed the grating that was supposed to be covering the shaft and tried to hide it under some rocks. You could see where someone cut the strapping that held the grating to some concrete poured around the shaft. I was looking around in the rocks to see if I could spot any more strapping, or even what it had been cut with, when I saw this." She looked back at Ryker. "I thought at first it was surveyor's tape, but when I realized it was a ribbon, I remembered that Charlotte had a pink ribbon in her hair Tuesday night at Mo's."

"The description you gave us didn't say anything about a pink ribbon," Travis said. He picked up a flyer from the corner of the table that held the stacks of maps. "This says Charlotte was last seen wearing a pink-checked sundress and pink sneakers."

Ryker frowned. "Right. She was wearing the pink ribbon the day before." He rubbed the side of his face. He was so tired he could scarcely feel his skin. "We need to ask my mom. She helps Charlotte with her clothes, though mostly Charlotte dresses herself."

Gage straightened. "I'll call her." He left the room.

Travis turned to Harper. "Did you see anything else suspicious or out of place at the mine? Any vehicles, or campfires, or signs that anyone had been there?"

She shook her head. "No. But I didn't go much farther than the mine shaft. I didn't explore the other ruins on the site."

Gage returned. "I talked to your mom," he told Ryker. "She's on her way over."

Wanda, dressed for church in a skirt and blouse and low heels, raced into the office five minutes later, her face flushed. She stopped short when she saw Harper. "Hello, Harper," she said.

"Hello, Wanda." Harper moved farther back in the room, clearing the space between Ryker and his mother.

Wanda turned to Ryker, her expression pleading. "They said you have something of Charlotte's you need me to identify."

"We need you to tell us if this really belongs to Charlotte," Gage said. He nodded to the ribbon on the table. "That."

Wanda walked over to the ribbon and started to pick it up, but Travis put out a hand to stop her. "It would be better if you didn't touch it," he said.

She nodded, and stared at the ribbon. "Yes, that's Charlotte's," she said after a moment. "I'm sure."

"When did she wear it last?" Gage asked.

"She wore it Tuesday. She had on a pink outfit that day." Her eyes grew shiny with unshed tears. "She wanted to wear it Thursday, too, but I told her it was wrinkled. I wanted to iron it before she wore it again." Her voice broke and she covered her mouth with her hand.

Ryker wanted to go to her, to put his arm around her and try to comfort her. But he couldn't really comfort her, and she was strong enough to get through this. So he sat, his hands clenched into fists, and suffered along with her. "I'll need you to check and see if the ribbon you remember is at your house," Travis said.

"It isn't." Wanda straightened her shoulders. "Thursday, after…after Charlotte went missing, I decided to iron the ribbon. So it would be ready when…when she gets back to us." She closed her eyes and breathed deeply. When she opened them again, her voice was steadier. "I thought I must have misplaced it. I've been so scattered. But now I wonder…" She stared at the ribbon. "Maybe Charlotte took it. She might have put it in her pocket, to show to a friend, or to wear later." She looked at Ryker. "You know how stubborn she can be about getting her way."

He nodded. "Yes. She's stubborn."

"Harper, why are you here?" Wanda had noticed Harper again.

"I found the ribbon," Harper said. "On a search and rescue call in the mountains."

"In the mountains? Where?"

"I'll explain later, Mom," Ryker said.

Gage stepped forward and placed the ribbon in a plastic evidence bag. "Did anyone besides you touch this at the scene?" he asked Harper.

She shook her head. "I put the ribbon in my jeans pocket to bring back down here. Do you think I destroyed evidence?"

"It's doubtful anything useful survived after being out in the elements for a few days, but we'll test it anyway," he said.

"We'll get a team up there to examine the area and see if we find anything else," Travis said.

Ryker stood. "Charlotte was up there," he said. "I'm right about Kim and Mick taking her into the mining district. They didn't go to Utah."

"If this ribbon really does belong to Charlotte, then yes, you could be right," Travis said.

Ryker knew the sheriff was being cautious. It didn't pay to jump to conclusions in criminal investigations. But he couldn't help feeling the sheriff was doubting him. "It's Charlotte's ribbon," he said again, proving his daughter wasn't the only one in the family who was stubborn.

Gage and the sheriff left the room. Wanda moved over to hug her son. "That ribbon is Charlotte's," she said. "We both know it."

He patted her back. "It is."

Then Wanda turned and embraced Harper. "Thank you

for bringing that to us. Anything of Charlotte's is precious to us."

Harper awkwardly returned the embrace. "I hope it helps," she said.

Wanda backed away. "I'd better go home," she said, and turned and all but ran from the room. Ryker suspected she would go off and cry somewhere where no one would see her.

"Your mother is such a nice person," Harper said.

"Yeah, she is. Charlotte being gone is killing her."

"It's awful for all of you. And I'm sure Charlotte misses you terribly. I could see how much she adores you."

He looked away, jaw clenched. Sometimes the only way he knew to cope was to think about anything but his little girl—what she must be doing right now. What she must be feeling. When he felt more in control, he turned back to her. "Will you take me to the place where you found the ribbon?" he asked. "After the crime scene investigators have done their work. Don't tell anyone. I'm probably not supposed to be up there, but I have to go."

"Of course you do. I'll go with you any time you're ready." Her eyes met his, such tenderness there that he felt the protective wall he was building around his emotions threaten to crack. She had always had a knack for seeing past any screen he tried to hide behind.

Chapter Eight

"I borrowed this Jeep from my folks," Ryker said when he picked up Harper for their drive to the Ida B Mine Monday afternoon in a red Rubicon. He had called midmorning to tell her the sheriff's department had found nothing of significance in their investigation of the site, and they were free to make their own visit. She had rushed to her apartment over her lunch hour and grabbed a change of clothes and a daypack. At the end of the day, she changed out of her dress and heels into jeans and hiking boots in the ladies' room at the office minutes before Ryker arrived. "I didn't think my car would make it up Stoney Gulch Road."

"It wouldn't," Harper said. "We barely got up it in the Beast—that's what we call the search and rescue vehicle. It has four-wheel drive and can go a lot of places regular cars can't go, but that road is really narrow. I was glad I was sitting in the back and couldn't see everything we had to navigate."

"Feel free to close your eyes on the way up," he said.

"I didn't used to be so nervous on those Jeep roads," she said. "But I've attended a few accidents now and heard enough stories about others that I know all the ways people get into trouble when they're just trying to have fun."

"How did you get involved with search and rescue?" he asked as they headed up the highway leading from town.

"I was living in Ohio and the company I worked for folded and I was out of a job. I was having a hard time finding a new one and my dad told me Taylor Geographic was looking for someone. I didn't want to have to depend on my parents for help, but I was getting desperate, so I interviewed for the job and was hired. I lived with my folks for six weeks until I got my own place, but in those six weeks I was restless and looking for excuses to get out of the house." She shook her head. "It's silly, I guess. But being back home, in the room I had since I was a little girl, unemployed and newly divorced—I felt like such a failure."

"I felt the same way when I moved back home with Charlotte," he said. "I needed help with her, but I felt like I was right back where I started. I'm starting to get over that. It would help if I had my own place, but you know what housing is like around here, and being in the same house with Mom and Dad really works better with Charlotte. Anyway, I didn't mean to interrupt. Tell me about search and rescue."

"The second week I was back I ran into Hannah Richards and she told me about volunteering with search and rescue and it sounded so, well, *important*. Not the sort of thing someone who was a failure would do. She invited me to an orientation class for new recruits and I liked what I heard. And it turns out, I'm pretty good at it. I don't panic and I'm good at pitching in to do whatever needs doing. And I really like helping others."

"That's great. It really is important work."

She angled toward him. "Now I want to know how you ended up as a cop."

"Don't sound so shocked. It's not like I was a juvenile delinquent."

"I would have thought after the way you were treated

following Aiden's disappearance, you wouldn't be the biggest fan of law enforcement."

"I mainly wanted to avoid cops," he said. "I got a degree in computer science but had a hard time finding a job after I graduated. Then my girlfriend, Kim, got pregnant and I had to find a way to support a family. The Fort Collins Police Department had a hiring fair and I picked up an application. The officer I talked to seemed like a good guy. The job had decent pay and benefits, so I decided to apply. I was shocked when they called to tell me to report to the police officer training academy." He frowned. "Kim laughed when I told her. She said she didn't know if she could stand being married to a cop."

"So you took the job because you didn't see another choice," she said.

"I thought so, but I ended up really liking the work." He slowed, searching for the turnoff to Stoney Gulch Road. "A patrol officer works alone much of the time. I had to learn to think on my feet, to act in a way that protected myself but also protected those around me. And even though I was working alone, I was part of a team of good officers who banded together to keep people safe and to prevent or solve crimes. There's a lot of variety. A lot to learn, too. And the paperwork is a pain. But I guess, like you with search and rescue, I discovered I'm good at the job. And I like making a difference."

"I wouldn't have laughed at you," she said.

"I know." He had spent too much of his marriage to Kim comparing her to Harper, or at least the ideal of Harper that he carried around in his head.

"I didn't leave because of what happened with Aiden," she said. "Or at least, that was one of the reasons my parents sent me away, but I never believed you had anything to do with his kidnapping."

He glanced at her, then back at the road. "I wondered. My lawyer told me I would find out who my friends really were, and when you left and I didn't hear from you…"

"My parents didn't give me a choice. I tried to get in touch with you, but my parents took my phone away, and my aunt didn't give me access to a phone or computer."

"I hoped that was the case," he said. "But it's good to hear you say it, even after all this time."

"I hated that I couldn't be there for you. And I hated more that you didn't know how much I believed in you."

"You're here now. That means a lot."

He made the turnoff onto Stoney Gulch Road and they immediately began to climb. The farther up they traveled, the narrower and rougher the road became, until he had slowed to five miles an hour, inching the Jeep over or around rocks and through deep ruts. "How much farther do you think it is?" he asked Harper, trying to gauge how many hours of daylight they had left. He didn't relish coming back down this road in the dark.

"Not much farther," she said. "The road ends at the mine and there's a flat space where you can turn around and park."

Fifteen minutes later he spotted the gravel apron that marked the end of the road. He parked and they got out. "That path leads to the mine." Harper pointed to an obvious trail as she slipped on a daypack.

He grabbed his own pack, locked the Jeep and they set out, Harper in the lead. The place was typical of other mountain mines he had visited, gray and red rock scraped bare of all but the most stunted vegetation, piles of waste rock and gravel spread around, bits of dried-up timbers, scraps of rusting metal, and the occasional old can or bottle the only testaments to what had once been a source of hope for the people who dug the shafts and searched for precious metals. Despite the barren landscape, the vividly blue sky and expansive views leant a wild beauty to the scene.

"The shaft is over here." Harper picked her way through loose rock to a metal grate approximately three feet square. Looking through the metal mesh, he could just make out the rocky sides of a shaft that extended into darkness. "Somebody said it was probably an air shaft, not an actual mine entrance," Harper said.

"Gage Walker said the mine entrance is a few hundred yards from here, and it's covered with an iron gate with a big padlock," Ryker said. "He said it didn't look like it had been disturbed." He nudged the grate with his toe and it shifted. "Why would someone cut off this grate?"

"I don't know." She turned to look along the small ridge they stood upon. "I found the ribbon over here."

He followed her to what looked like another pile of rock. "The grate was there." She pointed to a spot. "And the ribbon was about here." She looked down at their feet.

Ryker knelt and studied the ground. He didn't know what he had hoped to find that his fellow deputies or Harper hadn't already noted. There were no footprints. No blond hairs caught in the rock, nothing else to indicate a person had ever been here.

He rose again. "That ribbon couldn't have gotten up here unless Charlotte was here," he said. "Kim and Mick must have been here."

"It's a pretty desolate place to try to live," Harper said.

"Let's take a look around."

They followed a faint path away from the shaft, slightly downhill to the wooden frame and metal gate that marked the mine entrance. Peering inside, he could see a narrow hallway, not tall enough for him to walk upright, leading into the side of the hill. "Hello!" he shouted.

Only silence answered him. He examined the lock and his hand came away covered in orange rust. The lock, and the gate itself, looked as if they had been in place a long time.

They found a few old boards, some rusted cans and a no-trespassing sign full of bullet holes, but nothing to indicate Kim and Mick had spent any time here.

"There are a couple of other mines near here," Ryker said. "Let's see if we turn up anything there."

They walked back to the Jeep in silence. He tried to shrug off the heavy disappointment. It wasn't reasonable to expect to find anything where so many others had already looked. "I wonder," Harper said when they reached the vehicle. "Do you think Charlotte dropped that ribbon on purpose? As a clue, maybe?"

He stared. "What makes you think that?"

"You've read her stories, right? Little Red Riding Hood, leaving a trail of breadcrumbs in the woods?"

"I have. And we've gone hiking since she was a baby. I used to carry her in a pack on my back. I taught her to look for blazes on the trees to find the trail. We made a game of it and she loved spotting them before I did."

"You taught her a lot of useful skills she can use now," Harper said. "And she knows you're looking for her. I have no doubt of that."

"I hope she knows."

"You're a good dad," Harper said.

"I try. I read books and stuff, before she was born, but there's so much no one talks about. How the responsibility of having someone who depends on you totally is so heavy." He fit the key into the ignition but didn't start the Jeep. "I used to think about the baby you and I almost had. Would I have had any idea how to take care of him—or her—when I was so young?"

"She was a girl," Harper said.

An image of Charlotte as a newborn flashed into his mind. So tiny and fragile and utterly amazing. "I'm sorry I wasn't there for you," he said. "I should have—"

"Don't! Don't beat yourself up. We both did the best we could."

He started the Jeep. She was right. But that didn't really make him feel better.

He eased the Jeep back down Stoney Gulch Road to the highway, then turned off again a few miles farther on. The route here was not as rough, and led to a popular hiking trail. But before the trailhead was an unmarked turnout across bare rock to a claim that had been marked on the map as Sharp #8.

Long shadows stretched across the landscape by the time Ryker parked in front of what was left of the mine. "We can't spend much time here," he said. "But I'd like to look around."

"Sure." Harper turned in a half-circle, taking in the site, which had a few more trees than the Ida B Mine, stunted piñons bent by harsh winds and broken by heavy snow. A cabin formed of unchinked logs, silvered and hardened by a century or more of exposure to the elements, sat in the shadow of a hill, an orange-and-black no-trespassing sign affixed to the wall beside the opening for the door.

Ryker walked to the opening and peered in. The sharp, acrid tang of woodsmoke hit him. As his eyes adjusted to the dimness, he could just make out the remains of a campfire in the center of the room. "Someone has been here," he said as Harper moved up beside him.

He stepped over the threshold and pulled a small flashlight from his pocket and trained its beam on the fire ring. Someone had pulled a trio of stumps around a circle of rocks that formed the fire ring. He held his hand over the charred wood. It was cold. It could have been lit days or even weeks ago.

Harper moved slowly about the small room, examining the dried leaves, shells of piñon nuts, and other debris that littered the floor. She returned to Ryker's side with the wrapper from a stick of beef jerky and a crushed soda can. "I found these."

They were probably left by hikers who had stopped there for lunch, but he stuffed them in an evidence bag he had brought along just in case. He conducted his own survey of the little cabin, but found nothing.

When he and Harper stepped outside again, most of the daylight had faded. Ryker played the beam of the flashlight over the ground around the cabin and they walked as far as the mine opening, sealed by a metal gate. As they stood there, a trio of bats exited, and Harper jumped back with a squeak. "They startled me," she said, watching them flutter away.

"We'd better go," he said.

The Jeep bounced back down the narrow trail to the intersection of the Jeep road. He was preparing to turn when a vehicle sped past him, headed uphill at a reckless rate of speed. He braked hard to avoid being hit and stared after a white Jeep, its back end splattered with mud.

"There was a little girl in the back seat," Harper said. "A blonde. And a blonde woman in the passenger seat."

Ryker didn't hesitate, but turned to follow the other Jeep. The road quickly deteriorated, and they jounced over deep ruts and he jerked the wheel to avoid boulders that could have wrecked the vehicle. He gritted his teeth to keep them from slamming together at each jolt, and Harper clung to the dash with one hand and the strap hanging from the roof with the other. But no matter how fast he drove, the other Jeep was getting farther and farther away. He could barely make out the glow of its taillights in the distance.

They came to a section of road lined with three-foot boulders. He had to slow to a crawl to navigate through them. He could no longer see the other vehicle ahead. "I don't know how they're driving so fast," Harper said.

"They either know the road or they're being reckless," he said. "Probably a little of both."

"Where does this road go?"

"I think it ends at a trailhead, but I'm not sure. I've never driven it." Why hadn't he brought the maps with him? He had thought he could remember all he needed to know.

"If it ends, they'll have to stop and we can catch up with them then," she said.

They could, and what then? If the driver really was Mick, he was likely armed. Would Kim put Charlotte in danger? The thought made him cold all over, but it also made him keep driving. If the girl Harper had seen really was Charlotte, Ryker couldn't leave her with Kim and Mick.

He kept his speed down as the road climbed steadily. The moon rose, its light faint at first, then brighter. It painted the rocks in pewter shades. Some creature, dark and sleek, darted across the road in front of them and up into the rocks.

"There's the trailhead," Harper said.

A brown wooden sign listed the trails accessible from this parking area. A pit toilet sat at the far end of the lot, which was otherwise empty. "Where did they go?" Harper asked.

Ryker put the Jeep in Park, but didn't shut off the engine. He got out of the vehicle and turned to look in every direction. Was the other Jeep here, parked behind a boulder or an outcropping of rock? Moonlight drenched the landscape. Surely a white vehicle would stand out in all that light?

"I don't see anything," Harper said.

He walked to the edge of the parking lot. The ground dropped off sharply in a jagged cliff. No one had driven down there.

He moved to the trail. It was narrow, winding between boulders. No vehicle had passed this way, either.

He returned to the Jeep. "Let's go back the way we came," he said. "Maybe there's a turnoff we missed."

He found the turnoff a half mile back the way they had come. The narrow track was almost hidden by a rock outcrop, and was even rougher than the road they had traveled so far, carpeted with fist-size chunks of granite. Two hundred yards on, Ryker had to stop the car. "You wait here and I'll go ahead on foot," he said.

"Oh no you don't," she said. "The first rule of wilderness survival is 'don't separate from the group.' I'm coming with you."

He didn't argue, merely set out up the road, her walking behind. He had no trouble seeing the way in the moonlight, but he was also aware that they would be visible a long way before they approached wherever the Jeep had parked. They were taking a big risk, but the only alternative was leaving his daughter behind, and he couldn't do that.

"Look to your left," Harper whispered behind him. "There's something white behind those trees."

He slowly scanned to the left and spotted what she was talking about—a flash of something pale among the trees. "I've got to get closer to get a better look," he said. "But we need to pretend we haven't seen it, in case someone is watching."

"I'll follow you," she said.

He turned, and led the way back down the trail, as if they were returning to their Jeep. When they were out of sight of the clump of trees, he veered off into a boulder field. Trying to keep the largest rocks between him and the trees, he set an oblique, meandering path toward the spot.

They moved slowly, partly to avoid making noise and partly to keep from falling in the uneven terrain. He estimated it took the better part of an hour to circle around and come up on the other side of the trees. The pale object Harper had spotted was more visible now. It wasn't, as he had thought, the Jeep, but a tent. His heart beat faster as he realized he may have found what he was looking for—the place where Kim, Mick and—most important to him—Charlotte were staying.

"Wait here while I move closer," he whispered to Harper. "If anything happens to me, run back to the Jeep." He pressed the keys into her hand.

She nodded, eyes wide in the moonlight.

He crept forward, moving from bush to boulder, until he was on the edge of the clearing that contained the tent, a stack of firewood and a firepit lined with chunks of rock the same sandy red as the surrounding terrain. He paused, listening for any signs of movement inside the tent—the whisper of fabric as a body shifted in a sleeping bag, or the soft snoring of someone deep in slumber.

But the silence was absolute. It bothered him that he didn't know where the Jeep was. If they had followed the trail farther, maybe they would have found its parking place, but he would have felt better about approaching the tent and whoever was inside if he could have been sure of the vehicle's location.

He bent and scooped a handful of gravel from the ground at his feet, then straightened and hurled it toward the tent. It hit the side with a series of staccato patters.

No response. He repeated the gesture three times, waiting a full minute between each barrage, but no one stirred inside the tent. No one called out and no one emerged.

He took a step into the clearing, then another. He moved quickly after that, to the back of the tent. He drew out a knife and plunged it into the taut nylon fabric. The cut easily widened into an opening large enough for him to peer through.

The tent was a large cabin model, maybe eight feet square. Inside were three cots and several duffel bags, clothing spilling out of each. He played the beam of the flashlight over all of it, sorting out items suitable for a man, a woman and a little girl.

He stepped into the tent and went to the child's clothing. It was a smaller pile than the rest, only half a dozen items— shirts and pants and socks and underwear, all in Charlotte's favorite pink and purple. At the bottom of the pile was a pair of shoes. Pink tennis shoes with flowers stitched on the toes. The shoes Charlotte had been wearing the day she disappeared.

Chapter Nine

Harper waited in the dark for Ryker, focused on his silhouette moving around the campsite. What if whoever was in the tent pulled out a gun and shot him? What if it wasn't Kim and Mick at all, but someone else who didn't like someone creeping up on them in the middle of the night?

What if she was wrong and the little girl she thought she had glimpsed in the back of the white Jeep wasn't Charlotte at all? What if it was a little boy, or a dog, or a figment of her imagination, conjured up because she wanted so badly for Charlotte to be found?

But no, she had seen the girl. And she had definitely seen a blonde woman who could have been Kim. And the other vehicle had run away from them, as if wanting to escape.

She was sure she had never been anywhere so quiet. She sat on the ground behind a boulder the size of a compact car and the silence rang in her ears. She breathed in the aroma of sun-warmed rock and piñon and wondered what Ryker was doing right now.

The crunch of gravel set her heart to pounding, and she strained her eyes to see across the expanse of ground between here and the trees where the tent was staked. The moonlight washed everything into shades of gray and blurred the outlines like a monochrome impressionistic landscape.

Someone was coming. Someone tall and broad-shouldered, moving quickly and with confidence through the scattered rock. She relaxed and stood to meet Ryker as he drew near.

"They're gone," he said. "But they were here. I found Charlotte's shoes."

She wanted to cry out in frustration that they had been so close to the little girl, yet she had vanished again. "Where did they go?" she asked. "We were right behind them."

"We drove past this turnoff to the end of the road. They knew we were following them, so they probably waited until they were sure we were past and turned around and went back to the highway."

"Do you think they'll come back?" Harper asked.

"Probably not." He put his arm around her. "Come on. Let's go. As soon as we have a phone signal, I'll call the sheriff and let him know what I found. They can get someone up here to watch in case anyone returns. But my guess is they've moved on."

They trudged back to the Jeep, the walk seeming to take much longer now. Harper's feet dragged and her stomach growled. She wished she was home with her feet up, eating dinner and binging some mystery show on television, rather than being caught in the middle of a real-life mystery.

But then she focused on Ryker's broad back and felt guilty for those thoughts. When she left him, she could go back to her normal life, but he could never escape the reality that his daughter was missing.

They reached the Jeep and had to endure the slow, rough drive back to the county road, and another five miles on that road before they had a cell-phone signal. At last, Ryker pulled over at a scenic overlook and punched in a number. "Sheriff, this is Ryker. I've found where Kim and Mick were camping. They got away in a white Jeep. They covered the license plate with mud, so I couldn't read it. Charlotte is definitely with them. I found some clothes and a pair of her shoes at their camp."

He listened for a long moment, then gave directions to the camp. Then he hung up and turned to Harper. "If you want, you can call someone to pick you up. But I have to stay and take the sheriff and the crime-scene crew back to the campsite."

"I'll stay." Her stomach growled. "At least for a little while."

He leaned over the seat and pulled out a backpack. "I've got some protein bars and nuts in here."

"I've got a couple of apples."

They divided the food between them and ate. It wasn't the worst dinner she had ever had, and when she was done she was no longer hungry. In between bites, Ryker told her what he had seen at the campsite. "They had bought Charlotte some new clothes," he said. "And she had her own cot."

"So they're taking care of her."

"They're dragging her with them all over the mountains," he said.

She said nothing. Taking care of the child wasn't the same as doing what was best for her.

"The tent and all the camping equipment looked new," Ryker continued. "Which makes me wonder if they really planned this, or if it was a last-minute decision."

"If they didn't plan ahead, that could make it harder for them," she said.

"Harder for Charlotte, too."

"She knows you're looking for her."

"Does she? She's only four. What if they told her I wanted her to go with them?"

Harper didn't know what to say. He knew his daughter

better than she did. But she had been a little girl once, and he hadn't. "When I was Charlotte's age, I thought my father could do anything," she said. "He could climb mountains and fix cars and make pancakes and tell silly jokes, and he knew the names of the stars and the names of all our neighbors. If I had been lost or afraid or homesick, I would have believed he would come for me."

A vehicle approached and slowed. A black-and-white sheriff's department SUV pulled in behind the Jeep and stopped. Ryker switched on the Jeep's interior lights, then stepped out where he could be better seen. Harper lowered the window and waved. Sheriff Travis Walker got out of the SUV and moved toward the Jeep as a second sheriff's department vehicle turned in and parked. Seconds later, Gage Walker joined his brother and Ryker. "Three more deputies are on the way," the sheriff said. "Where is the campsite you saw?"

"I marked the mileage on our way out," Ryker said. "In three quarters of a mile, take a left onto the Jeep road that leads to a trailhead. Travel two point seven miles on that road. You'll see a big boulder on the left, and directly behind that boulder is a narrow dirt track. It's hard to see coming from this direction. That track ends at a clump of trees and in those trees is the campsite."

Travis looked past Ryker to Harper. If he was surprised to see her here, he gave no indication. "Did you see the camp, too?" he asked.

"I saw the trees and part of the tent, but I waited behind while Ryker went to investigate." She swallowed, suddenly nervous. "But I saw the white Jeep with Charlotte in the back seat, and Kim in the passenger seat."

"We'll need a statement from you later," Travis said. He returned his attention to Ryker. "Ride with me up to the camp so I can take a look. Then I'll bring you back here and the deputies will take over from there. You and Harper can come to the station tomorrow to give your statements."

Ryker turned to her. "I'm sorry you'll have to wait a little longer."

"It's okay." She took out her phone. "I've got a book on here I can read." She almost joked that she had been waiting for him for so many years, what was a few more minutes or hours? But she wasn't ready to admit that truth out loud. For so long she had told herself she was fine without Ryker in her life.

Until he was with her, and she realized she wasn't.

When Ryker finally returned home, he spent another restless night, anxious to know what evidence the deputies had found at the camp. Travis had ordered him not to return to the scene after he took Harper back to her place, so he had no choice but to go home and pretend nothing had happened. He was apparently a lousy actor, because his mother asked him what had happened to make him so agitated. He ended up telling her and his dad the whole story, meaning all three of them had slept little that night.

The next morning, he showered, shaved and put on his uniform, as he had been doing all week. Though he arrived at the sheriff's office before first shift began, Travis was already there. "What happened last night after I left?" Ryker asked.

"We took everything inside the tent for evidence," Travis said. "We left the tent in place and Declan is watching to see if they come back for their belongings. Wes will take over at nine."

"I can take a shift watching the tent," Ryker said.

"No you cannot. You're too involved already."

"You don't think I can remain professional?" Ryker asked.

"I'm not sure I could, if my kid was involved." Travis's tone softened. "I can tell by looking at you you've hardly slept since Charlotte disappeared. You're not in any shape to be out there in the field. I'm fine with you being here. I get it, you don't want to sit at home doing nothing. But you have to let the rest of us handle this."

He knew the sheriff was right. He also knew that Travis could have ordered him to go home and wait for them to call, and he appreciated that he hadn't done so. "All right," he said. "Thanks."

He returned to the conference room and the maps laid out on the table. He called up the aerial views of the terrain around the trailhead where they had turned around the night before, and found the little clearing where the tent had been. There was nothing there when these photos had been taken over a year ago, but he would have expected that. He looked through other photos and studied other maps, but his heart wasn't in the work anymore. Now that he knew Kim and Mick and Charlotte were close to Eagle Mountain, he wanted to be out there actively hunting them, not sitting here, helpless.

At noon Adelaide knocked on the door, then entered the room. She set a brown paper bag in front of him. "I made you a sandwich," she said. "I know you probably don't feel like eating, but think of it as something to do."

She left before he could even say *thank you*.

The sandwich was good, and she had included an apple and cookies she had probably made herself. He was reminded of the lunches his mother had packed for him when he was a child. The lunches she packed now for Charlotte.

As if summoned by the memory, he thought he heard his mother's voice down the hall. "I need to see Ryker. Please, where is he?"

"Mom?" He went to the door and was startled to see Wanda hurrying toward him, an envelope clutched in her hand. Gage followed her. She shoved the envelope at Ryker, her hands visibly shaking. "I went home at lunch and this was in the mailbox."

He took the letter, handling it by the corners, though it was already wrinkled where she had clutched it so tightly in her hand. It was addressed to him in a loopy cursive writing, with no return address. His stomach dropped. "It's from Kim," he said.

"I recognized her writing," Wanda said. "I remembered it from the wedding invitation she sent."

Gage inserted himself between them. He had slipped on a pair of latex gloves. "Let me open it," he said.

Ryker let Gage take the letter, and he and Wanda followed the sergeant into the conference room, where Gage shoved aside the stack of maps and dropped the envelope onto the flat surface. He teased open the flap of the envelope with a penknife and carefully removed the single folded sheet of notepaper inside. Ryker stared at the words Kim had written, confused.

Dear Ryker,
Charlotte is my daughter and you have no right to keep her from me. We're going to take good care of her. You need to stop looking for us. Mick will be a good father and he'll do whatever it takes to protect her, so don't mess with us.
Kim

Gage flipped over the envelope and examined it. "The postmark is Green River, Utah," he said.

"We know they're not in Utah," Ryker said. "They were here, just outside of Eagle Mountain last night."

"Are you sure? How good a look did you get at them?"

"I never saw them," he admitted. "I saw the backs of the heads of two people in a white Jeep, driving in front of me. But Harper saw them. She said she was sure there was a little girl who looked like Charlotte in the back seat of the Jeep, and a woman who looked like Kim in the front passenger seat. And Charlotte's clothes were in that tent."

"You said the clothes were new," Gage said. "That Kim probably bought them for Charlotte. Maybe they belonged to some other little girl."

"The shoes were Charlotte's. They were the pink ones with flowers on the toes that she was wearing when they kidnapped her."

Gage's expression was pained. "We checked and those shoes are really common. They're sold in discount stores all over Colorado."

"Sergeant, don't you think it would be an amazing co-incidence that a little girl who wore the same size clothing as my granddaughter, who owned the same shoes she was known to be wearing when she disappeared, who even fa-vored the same colors as her, was at that remote camp in the mountains? Especially when Harper Stanick is sure she saw Charlotte in that car."

"Coincidences happen." Gage rubbed his jaw. "I'm not saying you're not right about your ex and her boyfriend being here last night. But if that's the case, who sent this letter from Utah?"

"Green River is less than three hours from here," Ryker said. "They could have driven there to mail the letter, then come back. They've probably seen the news reports about the FBI looking for them in Utah and figured this was a good way to keep them on the wrong track."

"And you're sure this is Kim's handwriting?" Gage asked.

"Yes," they both answered at once.

"I'll need to show this to the FBI," Gage said. "They're going to say it supports their theory."

"You'll give the information about the camp I found, too," Ryker said.

"I will. But they might insist on taking over the investigation."

"I don't care who's in charge, I just want somebody to find Charlotte," Wanda said.

Gage nodded. "That's what we all want." He took out an evidence bag and eased the letter inside, then put the envelope in a second bag. "Let us know if you get any more letters. And we'll contact the post office in Green River and see if they know anything about who mailed the letter, though likely it was dropped in a mailbox somewhere."

He left the room and Wanda dropped into a chair. "I can't stand this," she said.

Ryker rested a hand on her shoulder, but said nothing. She looked up at him, eyes red, her mascara running. "When you were a teenager and you told us Harper was pregnant, I was so upset. Not only were you too young to be a father, I thought I was too young to be a grandmother. But over the next few weeks, I grew used to the idea, and I even felt a little excited. Then Harper left and we didn't know where she was, and later we found out she had lost the baby..." She shook her head. "What I'm trying to say is that by the time you told us Kim was pregnant, I was in a completely different place. I was over the moon, and I hated that the two of you didn't live closer so I could be more involved. I don't know if I've ever been as happy as I was the first time I held Charlotte. As much as I love you and your sister, I was even happier about Charlotte. You know I was never that wild about Kim, but I was determined to love her because she gave me that beautiful granddaughter." She covered his hand with her own. "Having the two of you here, living in the house with us, has been the best thing I could have imagined. I know one day you'll probably move away. I hope you find someone who can make you happy and be the mother Charlotte needs." She gave a hiccupy laugh. "I have so many dreams. But you know that now, don't you? It's what parents do."

"I know," he said. He had found himself imagining what Charlotte might be as she grew up, what great things she might accomplish.

"But right now all I want is for her to be safe and home again with us," Wanda said.

"We're going to find her," Ryker said. "We're going to bring her home."

Chapter Ten

Harper and Devlin were comparing notes about the resort project on Wednesday when Jacy, the receptionist, came in looking flustered. She hurried to Harper. "There are two men here who say they need to talk to you." She lowered her voice to a whisper. "They showed me identification that says they're with the FBI."

Devlin's eyes widened. "What have you done to have the FBI after you?" he asked.

Jacy scowled at him. "I don't think that's very funny. I put them in the client interview room next to Patterson's office," she said.

Harper followed her to the comfortably furnished lounge where clients could review the work the company had done for them or discuss new projects. "Are you Harper Stanick?" a craggy-faced man with very black hair and olive skin asked.

"Yes."

"Special Agent Cussler and Special Agent Reno."

"May I see some identification?"

They each displayed badges and ID. "Sit down." Cussler motioned to the sofa. "We have a few questions to ask you."

She sat, perched on the very edge of the sofa, in danger of sliding back on the marshmallow-soft cushions.

"We've received a report from the local sheriff's department about an incident in which you reported seeing Charlotte Vernon and her suspected kidnappers in a car near here," Cussler said.

"That's right."

"Could you describe the incident again for us, please," Agent Reno said. He smiled, while Agent Cussler's expression remained stern.

Harper described that evening again, until the point where Sheriff Walker and his deputies arrived. "Are you sure you saw Charlotte Vernon in that car?" Cussler asked.

"I saw a child with long blond hair who looked to be about Charlotte's age. And the woman in the front seat definitely looked like Kim Vernon."

"You know Kim Vernon?"

"I met her the night before Charlotte disappeared and spoke to her briefly. She's a very striking woman, not one I would forget."

"What about Charlotte Vernon? How well do you know her?"

"I met her that same night. She asked for my help washing her hands in the ladies' room. She is a very friendly, beautiful child."

"What is your relationship with Ryker Vernon?" Cussler asked.

The shift in the conversation startled her. "Ryker and I are friends."

"You're friends, but you only met his daughter for the first time the night before she disappeared?" Reno posed this question.

"I've only recently returned to town after living out of state," she said, determined to remain composed despite their firing questions at her. "Ryker and I ran into each other the day before—Tuesday. He was working an accident scene and I was part of the search and rescue crew called to help rescue the accident victims. Before then, we hadn't spoken in more than seven years."

"But you knew each other before?" Reno asked.

"Yes. We went to school together."

"So the two of you met at this accident and you saw him again the next night at Mo's Pub, is that the name of the place?" Cussler took over again.

"Yes. I was there with some friends and he was there with his daughter."

"So you didn't arrange to meet?" Cussler asked.

"No."

"You didn't think it was strange, seeing him again so soon?" Reno again.

"This is a very small town. It's not unusual to see people you know."

"Back to Monday afternoon," Cussler said. "This car drove past and you recognized Charlotte and Kim. Where was this exactly?"

"We were stopped at the end of a dirt road in the mountains, about to turn left onto another dirt road that leads back to the highway. We hadn't seen any other traffic all afternoon, but Ryker had to stop to wait for this car to go past."

"What kind of car?" Cussler asked.

"A white Jeep. I don't know what model. I don't know cars."

"How fast would you estimate it was going?" Cussler asked.

"Fast for travel on those rough roads, but not that fast overall. Maybe twenty-five miles an hour."

"What time of day was this?"

"About seven o'clock."

"Wasn't it too dark to see much in the car?" Reno spoke up again.

"It passed very close by. And there was plenty of light to see. It was dusk, not yet dark."

"Is it possible you saw someone else?" Reno asked. "Or imagined the child?"

"No. Why don't you believe me?"

Cussler moved closer. He was a tall man, looming over her. "Maybe you said you saw Charlotte because you wanted Ryker to like you better."

"I wanted… What are you talking about?"

"You say Ryker Vernon is your friend," Cussler said. "Why were you with him that afternoon?"

"I already told you I volunteer with search and rescue. While on a rescue call, I found a pink hair ribbon that belonged to his daughter. He wanted me to show him the place where I found the ribbon."

"Did you go with him to the campsite?" Cussler asked.

"Yes."

"Did you see the items he found in the tent—the child's clothing and shoes?"

"No. I waited outside the camp while he went to investigate."

"So you don't know if the items were there or if he put them there," Cussler said.

"Why would he put them there? And he wasn't carrying anything when he went up to the camp."

"He had a backpack, didn't he?"

"Yes, but it didn't have his daughter's clothing in it."

"How do you know?" Reno asked. "Did you look inside?"

She glared at both men. Before, she had been annoyed. Now she was getting angry. "Are you accusing Ryker of something?"

"We're not accusing anyone. But we have to consider all possibilities. What was his relationship with his ex-wife?"

"I don't think they had a relationship. He hadn't seen her since they divorced three years ago."

"You knew that or he told you that?" Cussler asked.

"He told me that but I've never known Ryker to lie."

"He didn't move to Eagle Mountain to get away from her?"

"He moved to Eagle Mountain so that his parents could help him care for his daughter. Why are you asking me all these questions about Ryker?"

"Why are you so upset?"

"I'm upset because a little girl is missing and you don't seem to be doing anything to find her."

Cussler stepped back. "That's all the questions we have for now. We may want to talk to you again. You can go now."

She was shaking as she walked out of the room and decided that instead of going back to her desk, she needed to get some fresh air and try to calm down. She crossed the street and walked two blocks to the park. The day was sunny and mild, a soft breeze stirring the broad leaves of the cottonwoods that towered over the park. A group of toddlers swarmed the playground in one corner, and a man played fetch with his dog on the grassy stretch in front of the stage where there were sometimes concerts in the summer.

She hadn't walked far before she saw a familiar figure ahead. "Ryker!" she called, and jogged to catch up with him.

He stopped and waited for her, hands in the pockets of his khaki uniform pants. "What are you doing here this time of day?" he asked.

"I needed some fresh air."

"Me too." A shriek went up from the playground and they

both looked over as a little boy slid down the slide, laughing all the way. "I never really noticed how many children are around, everywhere," he said.

"The FBI came to my office to interview me," she blurted. "They were horrible."

He stopped. "What did they do?"

"They practically accused you of having something to do with Charlotte's disappearance. They suggested you planted her clothing in that tent."

The lines around his mouth and eyes tightened. "I guess I shouldn't be surprised," he said. "They probably read about Aiden's case and the accusations against me."

"I told them you didn't have anything to do with Charlotte's disappearance."

They started walking again in silence. "I'm sorry I got you all tied up in this," he said after a moment.

"I'm not. I want to help."

"It helps just being with you. It was always like that, from when we first met."

"I was a little nervous about you at first." She smiled, remembering that first date. He took her to the local drive-in, having borrowed his father's car for the evening. "I didn't think you'd want to mess your hair up on a motorcycle," he had told her, and she had been both touched and disappointed. She had liked the idea of pressing up close to him, hanging on for dear life on the back of his motorcycle.

"Why were you nervous?" he asked.

She laughed. "Are you kidding? You were the cutest guy in our class. And you had that bad boy reputation."

"I thought you were the prettiest girl." He took her hand. "I still think you are."

She squeezed his hand, afraid to speak and break this spell. Then her phone buzzed. She sighed. "I'd better check that text," she said, and disengaged her hand from his. "It might be search and rescue."

It wasn't search and rescue, but Devlin. You okay?

I'm good, she replied. I just had to get some fresh air.

Good...bring me a latte when you come back?

She laughed, then showed the screen to Ryker. "I'd better get back to work," she said. "But I'm feeling better now."

"Me too."

She set off across the park toward her office, but at the street she stopped and looked back. He was still there, watching her. She waved and he lifted his hand in return. Of all the awful circumstances in which to fall in love with a guy, this had to be the worst, but then, she had always had a terrible sense of timing, from getting pregnant at seventeen to marrying a man she had known all of six weeks, to having to move back in with her parents at twenty-four.

What if Charlotte was never found? Or she was found and needed all of her father's attention to recover from her ordeal? Harper didn't see where she could fit in that scenario.

"Be careful," she whispered. She didn't want history to repeat itself. She had had more than enough of being hurt by Ryker Vernon.

RYKER WASN'T SURPRISED to find agents Reno and Cussler waiting to interview him when he returned to the sheriff's department after talking with Harper. "We have some questions about your alleged sighting of Kim Vernon and Mick Davis," said Cussler when the three of them were alone in one of the interview rooms. He was the older of the two agents and had the demeanor of someone in charge.

"All right." He reminded himself these men had the same goal he did—to find Charlotte and bring her home safely.

Cussler pulled out a chair and sat, while Reno stationed himself by the door. "How good a look did you get at the people in that Jeep you followed?" he asked.

"Not a very good look," he admitted. "The woman with me—Harper Stanick, I believe you've already spoken to her—told me she saw a child with long blond hair and a woman who looked like Kim in the vehicle."

Cussler's right eye twitched at the mention of Harper, or maybe it was the idea that Ryker already knew the feds had interviewed her, but he let the moment pass. "So it might not have been your daughter and your ex-wife in that car," he said. "It might have been two ordinary tourists."

"Except that we tracked them to a campsite with a tent that contained items I know belonged to my daughter."

"How do you know the clothing belonged to your daughter?" Cussler asked, his gaze drilling into Ryker, as if daring him to lie.

"I know my daughter's clothing."

"Do you?" Reno spoke for the first time. "I don't know mine. Except she has a lot of it."

"You probably have a wife to dress her," Ryker said. "I don't."

"You have a mother, though," Cussler said. "Isn't that why you moved here—so your mother could take care of your daughter?"

"I moved here so my parents could *help* care for my daughter. Especially when I have to be away at work. That doesn't mean I'm not the person primarily responsible for her." He leaned forward, his voice harder. "It's not a burden. I like spending time with her." If either of these men took this as a dig against their own parenting styles, so be it.

"Tell me more about the letter you received from your ex-wife," Cussler said.

Abrupt change of subject. A classic interviewing technique, designed to throw the suspect off guard. Was that how they saw him—as a suspect in his own daughter's abduction? "It was delivered to my parents' home yesterday," he said. "My mother found it and brought it to me here, at the sheriff's department."

"You recognized the handwriting?" Cussler asked.

"Yes. The handwriting looks how I remember Kim's. Though I haven't seen anything she's written in three years."

"The letter was postmarked from Utah," Cussler said.

"Yes. About a three-hour drive from here."

"So you think she drove all the way to Utah to mail a letter, then returned here?"

"Why not? She's probably heard the news reports that you guys think she and Mick and Charlotte are in Utah."

No eye twitch this time, but he gave Ryker a hard stare. "We'll be investigating this thoroughly."

"Did you check the items from the tent for fingerprints?" Ryker asked. "I know Mick's are on file."

"We know how to do our job, Deputy."

Ryker nodded. He wanted to believe this, but part of him couldn't help insisting that no one would work as hard to find Charlotte as he would.

"Tell us about Aiden Phillips," Cussler said.

Ryker had expected this, but the words still sent a chill through him. "Aiden was my cousin. I was babysitting him when he was taken from his room. His body was found two days later. I didn't have anything to do with his murder. I was cleared as a suspect."

"Because a neighbor provided a statement that the motorcycle you rode never left the front of the house the night Aiden disappeared," Reno said. "And you didn't have access to another vehicle."

"And my DNA wasn't a match for that found on Aiden's body."

Reno looked away. Cussler shifted, the chair creaking beneath his weight. They would have known the facts in Aiden's case before they brought it up. They were purposely trying to unsettle him. "You said you haven't spoken to your ex-wife in three years," Reno said. "She had no contact with you or with your daughter in that time?"

"No."

"Why do you think she came to Eagle Mountain now? Why take your daughter?"

He had lain awake nights thinking about this question. "I don't know," Ryker said. "But when Kim left she said that once she and Mick were 'settled' she would come back for Charlotte."

"What was your response to that?" Reno asked.

"I didn't say anything," he said. "I intended to ask for sole custody of Charlotte—I didn't want a felon like Mick Davis to have anything to do with her. But I was also hoping Kim and I could work out some sort of visitation arrangement so that Charlotte could still see her mother."

"That seems very generous, seeing she abandoned you both," Cussler said.

"I would have been fine with never seeing her again," Ryker said. "But I had divorced friends who used their children to get back at their exes. It was ugly and I'm convinced it hurt the children. I had other friends who worked things out amicably and I saw how much better that was for the children. I wanted to do what was best for Charlotte."

"But Kim never took you up on the offer of visitation?" Cussler asked.

"She never contacted me again," he said. "I had to hire

a private detective to track her down to deliver the divorce papers, and even then she didn't ask about Charlotte."

"Did that surprise you?" Cussler asked.

"Yes and no. For all her faults, I thought she was a good mother. But she was also...unpredictable. And once she and Mick started seeing each other, it was like she was obsessed. She didn't want to have anything to do with anyone but him."

"Do you believe he manipulated her?" Cussler asked. "Do you think he's behind the abduction?"

"I don't know. I probably haven't spoken ten words to him in my life. Though I can't say he ever showed any particular interest in Charlotte before. And Kim told me once that he didn't want children. I always believed that was why she hadn't tried to be involved with Charlotte's life."

"I wonder what changed," Reno said.

"I don't know." Ryker looked at the younger agent. "You probably know more about Mick than I do. I've read his rap sheet, but that's it. Is there something I should know?"

The look that passed between the two agents sent an icy surge up Ryker's spine. "What?" He leaned forward. "What aren't you telling me?"

"You don't need to be concerned," Cussler said, but while he was probably practiced at deceiving suspects, Ryker immediately knew he was lying.

"You need to tell me," Ryker said, barely managing to keep his voice even. "We're talking about my daughter."

Cussler wouldn't meet his gaze. He pushed back his chair and stood. "You're free to go now. We'll be in touch if we need anything else."

Ryker stood also, hands in fists at his sides. He wanted to grab the man across from him and shake him—to force him to reveal whatever he knew about Mick Davis. But that wouldn't get him anywhere, except perhaps arrested.

He left the room and stood in the hallway for a long moment, trying to slow his breathing and calm his racing heart. He tried to think of who might help him. Sheriff Walker had been sympathetic—a man with two young children of his own. But the sheriff was also a man who played by the rules. He had taken over a department that had a history of scandal and made sure there was nothing like that associated with his watch.

He headed for the office across the hall from the sheriff's. Gage Walker looked up from his desk. "Finished with the feds?" he asked.

Ryker stepped inside and closed the door. "I need a favor," he said.

"Let's hear it."

"The feds know something about Mick Davis that they won't tell me. I think maybe something to do with his history with children, a crime involving a child, something like that. They know I can find anything on his rap sheet, but maybe he's a suspect in some crime involving a child— something I can't uncover. They didn't come right out and say it, but they implied that he might be the one behind Charlotte's kidnapping, not Kim."

"And you want me to see what I can find out," Gage said.

"Yes."

"If it's not good, it's only going to make you feel worse," Gage said. "It's not going to make him easier to find."

"No. But my daughter is with him. I need to know."

Gage looked as if he wanted to dispute this. "If it was your daughter, wouldn't you want to know?" Ryker asked.

Gage blew out a breath. "Yeah." He looked at his computer. "I'll do some digging, let you know what I find."

"One more thing." Ryker didn't wait for Gage to answer, but pushed forward. "I want to see the file on Aiden Phillips's disappearance."

"Do you think Mick Davis had something to do with that?"

"No. But I want to see what evidence investigators collected at the time. Maybe I'll spot something they overlooked, or a new lead to follow."

"You were a suspect in that case."

"But I was cleared. My DNA wasn't a match."

"Do you really think you'll find anything?" Gage asked.

"Probably not. But I want to try. Even though my DNA wasn't a match, there are still people who believe I had something to do with Aiden's death. Those people aren't going to be satisfied until someone else is proven guilty." At Gage's doubtful look, he added, "I'm officially on leave and I can't drive around searching for Charlotte twenty-four hours a day. Going over Aiden's case will give me something else to focus on."

"I'll have to dig it up out of the archives," Gage said.

Ryker stood. "Thanks. I'm going to go home now. You can contact me there."

"Just one thing," Gage said. "Whatever I find out about Davis, you have to promise me you won't do anything rash. It won't help Charlotte and it will only hurt you."

Ryker nodded. His head knew this was true. His heart, on the other hand, wasn't so sure. If Mick or anyone else hurt Charlotte, he didn't know what he might do. He was her father. His job was to protect her. If he couldn't do that, did anything else really matter?

Chapter Eleven

Seven years ago.

Ryker hesitated when he stepped out of his house, a deputy on either side. He had known a crowd had gathered outside his parents' home, but he hadn't been prepared for the number of people who suddenly crowded around him, or their animosity. Some shouted his name as the deputies hurried him toward the black-and-white cruiser waiting at the curb, while others yelled accusations and questions. "What did you do to Aiden?"

"Where is Aiden?" Others carried homemade signs with words like *Murderer!* or *Confess!* The sight shook him.

His father and the lawyer, Mr. Shay, walked behind him. His mother had stayed behind, barely keeping it together.

"Don't look," Shay said when Ryker started to turn his head toward the crowd.

One deputy put a hand on top of Ryker's head and pushed down, guiding him into the back seat of the cop car. They hadn't cuffed him. "You're not under arrest," one deputy had said, but they hadn't said coming to the station and answering more questions was optional, either.

At the sheriff's department, more people had gathered. Reporters, too. They pushed forward with microphones, cameras flashing, and shouted more questions—at him, at his father and at the deputies. No one said anything, their expressions stony.

Except Ryker. Later, when the pictures ran in the paper and on television, everyone could see how frightened he was. He was eighteen, but he looked younger.

They led him to the same room where they had questioned him before. His lawyer sat beside him. Ryker retold the story of everything that had happened that night, just as he had before.

"Tell us what you did with Aiden," the sheriff demanded. "Tell us where he is."

"I don't know where he is," Ryker answered. "I didn't do anything to him."

The sheriff, a craggy-faced man with a gray buzz cut who smelled of cigarette smoke, stalked back and forth in front of Ryker. "We know you killed him," he growled. "When we find his body, we're going to find the evidence that you did this."

A knock on the door interrupted them. Urgent whispering, then the sheriff and the two deputies left. Ryker looked at Shay. "They don't believe me," he said. "I would never hurt Aiden. He's a great kid."

Shay squeezed his hand. "I know this is hard," he said. "Just hang in there. They're trying to frighten you. They don't have any evidence."

The door opened and the sheriff returned. "We found Aiden," he said.

Hope flared in Ryker's chest. "Is he alive?"

"You know he isn't. We found his body where you left him. You should make it easy on yourself and tell us what happened right now. We're going to get DNA evidence from the scene. It's going to be a match. Then it's going to be all over for you."

"My client doesn't have anything more to say," Shay said. "He's already told you everything he knows."

The sheriff's face grew redder. He shook his head and left the room. Shay stood. "Come on, Ryker. Let's get you home."

Ryker glanced at the deputies. One was looking at the wall, but the other glared at him. *He really thinks I'm a murderer*, he thought.

Shay put a hand on his arm and Ryker stood and followed him out of the room. No one tried to stop them.

Ryker's dad joined them. He hugged Ryker. "They found Aiden," Steve said.

"I know." Ryker tried to swallow tears, but the knot in his throat wouldn't go down. His voice broke. "They said he's dead."

Steve nodded. Tears streamed down his face and seeing that made Ryker cry, too. Shay led them outside to the car. Inside, away from the reporters and the shouting people, Ryker pulled himself together. "What's going to happen now?" he asked.

"We'll wait for the DNA to come back," Shay said. "That will point to Aiden's real killer."

"Who would want to hurt him?" Ryker asked. "He was a great kid. I thought that night—I just found out my girlfriend is pregnant. I thought how great it would be to have a little boy like Aiden as my son."

Steve put an arm around Ryker's shoulders and pulled him close. Neither of them spoke—they didn't have to.

It took three weeks for the DNA results to come back. Three weeks of crowds in front of the house, shouting and waving their signs. Someone at the sheriff's department had told a reporter that Ryker was the only suspect. His mom had to take a leave of absence from her job after someone called her boss and berated her for keeping a murderer's mother on staff. Someone keyed his father's truck and wrote an obscenity on the window.

Aiden's parents asked the family not to attend Aiden's funeral, as it would be too upsetting.

When the sheriff called a press conference to announce the DNA found on Aiden's body was not a match to any known person, most of the attention died down. But Harper didn't return to town, and people still stared and whispered when Ryker walked by. As soon as he graduated, his parents suggested he visit his cousins in Texas. Ryker left, though he felt like he was running away. He left because it would be easier on his parents. He thought he would stay away until they found Aiden's killer. Except they never did.

HARPER HAD POURED her first cup of coffee Thursday morning when she received a text from search and rescue. All available volunteers report to Ruby Falls to search for missing child. Her breath caught as an eerie sensation of déjà vu swept over her. Another missing child? Or had Charlotte been spotted in the Ruby Falls area, triggering this new search?

She finished dressing, then left a message for her boss that she had been called out on a search. As she headed for her car, she dialed Hannah Richards. "Who is the missing child?" she asked as soon as her friend answered the phone.

"I don't know any more than you do," Hannah said. "I guess we'll find out when we get there."

The summons had brought out the full contingent of SAR volunteers, veterans and trainees alike. Harper followed a line of familiar vehicles up Dixon Pass, toward a section of red rock cliffs that flanked the highway. The steep cliffs were prone to avalanches after heavy snows, but this time of year they were merely one more section of stunning scenery along the winding mountain road.

She parked behind Christine Mercer's blue RAV4 at a trailhead a few hundred feet from the falls, just behind a trio of yellow-and-black barriers that closed the road to traffic. Beyond the barriers, lights from several law enforcement SUVs, a wrecker, and an ambulance strobed off the cliff walls. A dark gray SUV was snugged up against the rocks, its front end smashed in, all four doors open. Paramedics were transferring someone to a litter as Harper joined the others around Captain Danny Irwin.

Danny hoisted his lanky frame atop a square of granite that had fallen from the cliffs years ago and now served to mark the edge of the narrow shoulder where some of the emergency vehicles were parked. He surveyed the gathered volunteers, who fell silent, waiting to learn the details of their mission.

"We're searching for a five-year-old boy, Noah," Danny said. "He and his parents were in that vehicle when someone ran them off the road and they crashed into the cliffs."

They all looked toward the smashed-up SUV. "His mother, the driver, sustained injuries in the crash and was trapped in the car. The father had some more minor injuries, but he says Noah was unhurt. Because the car was partially in the road, the father was concerned they might be hit from behind by another car, so he got Noah out and took him to about here and had him climb up in the rocks a little, where he'd be out of the way. Dad told Noah to stay put, then went to check on his injured wife. He called 911 and sheriff's deputies and paramedics responded. Deputy Ellis remembers seeing Noah waiting by the side of the road here when he arrived, but by the time firefighters began cutting up the SUV to allow access to his injured mom, he had disappeared."

A buzz of conversation rose from the volunteers, but died down again when Danny raised his hand. "Anna and her search dog, Jacquie, are on their way, but she was in Junction when the call went out, so we'll start without them. Noah is four feet tall, weighs forty-six pounds and has light brown hair and hazel eyes," he said. "He's wearing blue sweatpants and a green T-shirt and blue tennis shoes."

"He probably saw something that distracted him, he went to investigate, and he got lost," Carrie Stevens said. "That's the kind of thing my son would do."

Danny nodded. "I thought of that, too." Harper remembered that Carrie and Danny lived together, and she had two children from a previous relationship. "Pair up and spread out," he directed. "I want three teams on the three hiking trails that branch off from the trailhead where some of us parked. The rest of you, search both sides of the road. Climb up or down where you can, but be careful. Look for anything that's disturbed—rocks overturned, a child's footprint, anything he might have dropped. And be careful. Any questions?"

Caleb Garrison stuck up his hand. "You said someone ran them off the road? Do they know who?"

Deputy Shane Ellis had moved to stand beside Danny. "The dad described a white Jeep, traveling at a high rate of speed. It was northbound and came around the curve in the southbound lane. The mother had to swerve to avoid hitting it, skidded on the gravel and slammed into the cliff."

Harper winced. "I take it the Jeep didn't stop," Danny said.

Shane shook his head. "It didn't stop, and the dad doesn't remember any other cars passing by immediately after the accident. One man stopped after the dad called 911, but once he heard help was on the way, he continued on."

"Noah hasn't responded to his father's or the deputies' calls for him," Danny said. "He may have fallen, or he might simply be afraid of strangers. Keep those things in mind as you search. Good luck."

Harper teamed up with Christine and they began their search along the shoulder of the highway opposite the cliffs. The shoulder was only about a foot wide here, with no guardrails, and a steep drop-off into a deep canyon. Harper kept her eyes focused on the rough terrain below. "Would a little boy try to climb down those rocks?" she asked Christine. "It's so steep."

"Maybe," Christine said. "I mean, some kids are pretty fearless. Still…" Her voice trailed away as they looked down the long, steep slope. Harper didn't want to think about what could happen if Noah slipped on a loose rock, or lost his balance and went tumbling.

"I hope they find whoever was driving the car that ran them off the road and file charges," Christine said as they continued slowly along the shoulder. "The speed limit is twenty-five miles per hour in this section for a reason."

"There are a lot of white Jeeps around," Harper said. But even as she spoke, an image flashed into her mind of the white Jeep she and Ryker had followed on that mountain backroad—the one they were sure contained Kim, Mick and Charlotte. They had been driving much too fast, as well. Was it possible this was the same Jeep?

"Noah!" Christine cupped her hands around her mouth and shouted. The name echoed back at them, but they heard no reply.

They moved on to a rock outcrop that jutted from the shoulder, forming a small platform just big enough for a person to stand on. But currently, the platform was occupied by a yellow-bellied marmot. The furry rodent, as big as a house cat, was flattened on its belly in the sun. It sat up at their approach, but made no move to run away. "Seen a little boy around here?" Christine asked.

The marmot blinked, and let out a high-pitched squeak. Christine took a step toward it and it dove off the side of the platform and disappeared between the rocks below. Harper moved closer to see if she could spot where the marmot had gone, but another movement farther down the slope distracted her.

"Noah!" she shouted.

Christine hurried to her side. "What is it?" she asked. "Do you see something?"

"Down there, under that tree. Does it look like a person to you?" A small person, with blue sweatpants and tennis shoes, lying very still. "Noah!" she shouted again, unable to keep the frantic note from her voice.

Other volunteers gathered around them. Danny moved in, binoculars in hand. Harper held her breath, still staring at the figure far down the slope. Danny lowered the binoculars. "I think it's him," he said. "And I think I saw him move."

Everything happened very quickly after that. A team began rigging ropes to descend to the boy, while others gathered safety gear and first aid supplies. Tony and Danny consulted on the best way to bring up the boy, depending on his injuries. "I'll climb down to him," Ryan said.

"Let me go first," Sheri said. "He might be less afraid of a woman."

"You'll both go," Danny said. "It will take two of you to get him safely into the litter."

Sheri descended first, rappelling the last third of the way down what looked to Harper like a straight drop. Ryan followed and met her at the base of a small tree, which had apparently stopped Noah's fall.

"Let me through, please." A brown-haired man in his thirties, with a bandaged head and blood-splattered clothing, pushed between the volunteers. "I'm Noah's dad," he said. "Have you really found him?"

Danny put a hand on the man's arm, as if to hold him back. "Our volunteers are checking him out and figuring out how best to bring him up."

The man stared down at the scene below. Noah was hidden by Sheri and Ryan as they bent over his body. "Please tell me he's not dead," he whispered.

Danny's radio crackled. He turned to Harper, who was closest. "You stay with Mr. Ericson," he said. "Look after him." Which she took as code for *Don't let him do anything stupid.*

Danny walked away and Harper moved in next to Mr. Ericson and wondered if she should try to distract him. "You look like you were injured in the accident," she said. "Are you okay?"

"I'll be okay when my boy is safe." His eyes never wavered from the scene below.

Danny returned, looking less tense than before. "Sheri and Ryan say Noah is conscious and talking to them. He said he went over to look at a marmot and slipped and fell. They think he may have a broken arm, and he bumped his head, so that will have to be checked out. But he's lucid and his vital signs are good. They're going to stabilize the arm and get him into a helmet and secured in the litter and bring him up."

"Thank God." Mr. Ericson staggered and Danny and Harper steadied him on either side.

"Why don't you sit down," Danny said. "You can see

Noah as soon as they bring him up." He helped lower the man to the ground. "Stay with him," he said again to Harper.

She sat beside Mr. Ericson. "Noah will have a great story to tell for the rest of his life," she said. "About the time he slid off a mountain and got hauled up by search and rescue."

"His mom used to joke about putting a leash on him. He's such a live wire. Just so interested and curious about everything."

"He's going to be okay." She hoped that was true. Children were resilient, right? "How is your wife?" she asked.

"Shattered kneecap, sprained wrist and some cuts on her face from broken glass. She'll be okay." He glanced over his shoulder, but from this vantage point, they couldn't see the wreck. "The car is totaled, of course. Not that that matters. As long as my family is safe."

"I understand another car ran you off the road?"

"A white Jeep. It came flying around the curve in our lane, going way too fast. My wife had to swerve to avoid it. Next thing I know, we slammed into that wall. We weren't going very fast, but still." He shook his head.

"Did you get a look at the driver?"

"It was a man, but I couldn't tell you more than that. And there was a passenger. A woman, I think."

"Anyone else? Any children?"

"I don't know. It happened so fast."

A cheer went up and Harper and Mr. Ericson both stood in time to see Noah, cocooned in the litter, an orange safety helmet almost obscuring his face, start up the slope. Less than five minutes later, the litter slid onto the shoulder of the road. Mr. Ericson hurried to see his son. "Daddy!" Noah said, and squirmed.

Mr. Ericson knelt beside the litter. "Just be still," he said.

"You're going to get to ride in the ambulance. We'll go see your mom."

"Is Mama okay?"

"She's going to be just fine. She'll meet us at the hospital."

Paramedics moved in to take over and Harper turned away. She walked back down the road, toward the wreck site. A wrecker was hooking onto the SUV, leaving a trail of broken glass and metal behind. She looked down the road, trying to picture the scene Mr. Ericson had described, the white Jeep barreling toward them.

"He's lucky she steered toward the cliff and not the canyon."

Gage Walker joined Harper in watching the wrecker. "He said it was a white Jeep, with a man and a woman in the front seat," Harper said. "He didn't know if there was anyone else in the car."

"There are a lot of white Jeeps in the country," Gage said. "And there's nothing unusual about a couple in a car."

"Ryker and I saw Kim and Mick in a white Jeep with Charlotte," she said. "They were driving very fast for the roads we were on."

"We're looking for them," Gage said. "And we'll look for this vehicle too, but we don't have much to go on."

She looked up at him. "Do you believe that I saw Kim and Mick and Charlotte?"

"Yes."

"I'm not sure the FBI did."

"They're practiced at not revealing anything they're thinking," he said. "That doesn't mean they don't believe you. But it's a good idea to remain skeptical. Some people do lie."

"I know it was Kim and Charlotte I saw. I didn't get a good look at the driver, but I think it was a man, and we know Kim has been traveling with Mick."

"No one is giving up on finding them," Gage said. "A lot of people—law enforcement and regular citizens like you—are still looking."

"The FBI think they're in Utah."

"They're looking in Utah, but I think they're looking here, too. They talked to Ryker for a long time yesterday afternoon."

"He's a fellow law enforcement officer. Did they tell him anything? Do they have any leads?"

"I don't think so."

She looked around at Deputy Ellis and Jake Gwynn talking with Hannah and a couple of other search and rescue volunteers. "Where is Ryker now?" she asked.

"He went home. I think being at the sheriff's department, knowing we weren't getting anywhere with our search, was getting to be too hard on him."

"He's not going to feel any better sitting at home, missing her."

"No. But he can be with his parents. I think they need him now."

"This must be so horrible for them all."

"You should stop by and see them. They would probably appreciate it."

"You mean, like, take a casserole?" That was what people did in a crisis, wasn't it—take food?

"I doubt Ryker is interested in casseroles, but he might appreciate a friend to talk to."

Right. But nothing she said was going to make him feel better. Only getting Charlotte back would do that.

A RESERVE DEPUTY arrived at Ryker's house midmorning on Thursday with a box Ryker was required to sign for. Ryker took the box upstairs to the room he used as a home office and lifted the lid. Stacks of folders and envelopes, each labeled with a seven-digit case number, half-filled the space. This was supposedly everything related to Aiden Phillips's disappearance.

Ryker removed the contents and began flipping through them. Some photos of the open window and the ground beneath it, as well as Aiden's room, and his empty bed. Transcriptions of the interviews with Ryker, which he didn't bother to read. He also set aside the envelope labeled Body Photos.

He came to a sheaf of papers identified as an interview with Margery Kenner, and settled in to read. With the precision of the school teacher she had been for so many years, Mrs. Kenner described her interaction with Ryker immediately after he discovered Aiden was missing. "He was really upset. Frantic," she said.

"He didn't do anything to harm Aiden, I'm sure of it," she added. "I saw them playing ball earlier that evening. Ryker was good with him. Patient. He never left the house that night."

When pressed, she explained that Ryker's motorcycle was loud and he parked it in front of Aiden's house, directly across from her bedroom window. She hadn't slept well and had the window open. "I would have heard him if that motorcycle had moved an inch. And how is he going to carry a little boy on a motorcycle anyway? It's ridiculous."

He smiled, picturing Mrs. Kenner berating the deputy. When asked if she had seen anyone else near the Phillipses' house that night, she said, "Only one vehicle went down the street, a red Ford pickup." She said she thought the truck might belong to a local handyman, Gary Langley. He had repaired her porch the week before, so she remembered the truck, but she couldn't be sure it was his. He lived on the other side of town.

A chill shuddered through Ryker. Langley was the old man who had approached him outside the sheriff's department the night Charlotte was kidnapped. Even in a small town, it was an eerie coincidence.

He searched through the file to see if the sheriff's department had ever interviewed Langley. He found a brief mention of the man in a report: "Mr. Langley said he was not in the Phillipses' neighborhood that night, and in any case, he sold the truck a week prior, to a man in Texas."

Ryker frowned. He could find nothing in the files to show that anyone had followed up to verify the date of the sale of the vehicle, or any explanation of why it had been sold to someone out of state.

There was nothing else of interest, so he turned to his laptop and did a search for Gary Langley. He found a dozen references, none of which seemed related to the handyman.

The doorbell rang and Ryker tensed, and listened as his dad answered the door. "Harper! Come in! It's good to see you."

Ryker made it to the top of the stairs in time to see his father embrace Harper. His mother entered the picture and she too hugged Harper. "Come in and have some coffee. Or a soft drink or tea?" His mother took Harper's hand and pulled her toward the kitchen.

"Hello, Harper."

She stopped and looked up, and he felt the impact of her gaze like a physical touch. "Hello Ryker. I hope you don't mind me stopping by."

"Of course not." He hurried down the stairs to meet her.

"I can't stay long," Harper was telling his parents when

he joined them in the kitchen. "I just wanted to see how you were all doing. And talk to Ryker for a minute."

"We're all pretty miserable, as you can imagine." Wanda released Harper's hand. Steve moved to put his arm around her. "Ryker told us you saw Charlotte in that Jeep when you two were in the mountains. Did she look okay?"

"She looked fine. I mean, I only caught a glimpse of a girl with long blond hair in the back seat of the vehicle."

"Was she in a car seat?" Wanda asked. "We always make sure she's in her booster seat whenever we're in the car."

"I... I don't know." Harper sent Ryker a desperate look.

"Come on upstairs," Ryker said, and turned to lead the way.

Harper followed him. Behind them, he could hear his father softly talking to his mother, probably telling her to leave the two of them alone. He understood she was desperate for any positive news about Charlotte, but her obvious pain was tough to deal with, especially for someone as empathetic as Harper.

"You're not working today?" he asked when they reached the landing at the top of the stairs.

"I'm supposed to be. I got called out for search and rescue early this morning, so I'm late getting to the office. I just stopped by for a few minutes to tell you about the call."

He tensed. She hadn't stopped by just to shoot the breeze about a traffic accident or a lost hiker. "What was the call?"

"A missing little boy."

She must have read the horror on his face, because she rushed to add, "It's okay. He had just wandered away from his parents and slipped and fell. A tree stopped his fall and he probably broke his arm, but he's going to be fine."

"That's good." He never wanted to see his daughter hurt, but if she came away from this ordeal with nothing more than a scare and an arm that would soon mend, he would be relieved. "So what did you want to tell me?"

She glanced over her shoulder toward the bottom of the stairs. They could still hear the murmur of his parents' conversation. "Is there some place more private we can talk?" she asked.

"Come in here." He led her to the room he had set up as a home office, with a desk and computer. Her gaze immediately fixed on the smaller desk adjacent to his. "Charlotte likes to color or pretend to do schoolwork while I'm busy on the computer," he said. He had to force the words past a knot in his throat.

Harper faced him, her back to the desk. "The little boy belonged to a couple who were injured in a car accident. They were southbound near the Ruby Falls section of Highway 60 when a white Jeep came around the curve and crossed in their lane. The woman, who was driving, swerved to avoid a head-on collision and ended up slamming her SUV into the cliffs. Fortunately, they all should recover from their injuries."

"A white Jeep. Did they see who was driving?"

"They said a man was driving, with a woman passenger. They couldn't see into the back seat. It all happened very quickly. But I remembered how fast the Jeep we saw was going, despite the rough road."

He rubbed the back of his neck. "There are a lot of white Jeeps. It could be a coincidence."

"Or it could be Kim and Mick." She rested her hand on his shoulder. "Anyway, I thought you'd want to know. I wish I could do more to help."

He wanted to lean into her touch, to let someone else take part of the weight he was carrying. "You are helping," he said. He covered her hand with his own, holding her there, close to him. "I'm glad we're friends again. I've missed you."

"I've missed you, too."

"Do you think about her? Our daughter?" The little girl they might have had together had been on his mind lately, another lost child of his.

"I do," she said. "I wonder what she would look like. What she would be like."

"Yeah. Sometimes I wish things had worked out differently."

"Then you wouldn't have Charlotte."

"No." But he might have had two daughters. Who knew?

She moved away, breaking the tie between them. The physical one, anyway. Their past connected them, no matter what happened in the future. "I have to get back to work," she said.

"Thanks for stopping by."

"You know you can call me anytime. I mean it."

"I know." But was that the right thing to do—make her share in this sorrow, when she had already endured plenty of her own?

"I'll see myself out."

He stood there until he heard the front door close softly behind her. His phone rang and he answered it. "You need to get down here," Gage said, his voice clipped. Grim. "There's been a development."

Chapter Twelve

Gage refused to elaborate, only repeated that Ryker needed to come to the sheriff's department as soon as possible. He was waiting when Ryker arrived and pulled him into an empty conference room. "What's going on?" Ryker asked, searching Gage's expression for any clues, but finding none. "Have you found Charlotte? Is she okay?"

"We haven't found Charlotte," Gage said. "But Dwight is bringing in Kim. She flagged down a Jeep up past Galloway Basin. When the driver heard who she was he had sense enough to call 911."

A rush of adrenaline staggered Ryker. "Kim was by herself? Where are Charlotte and Mick?" He clenched his fists to keep from grabbing Gage by the shoulders and shaking the answers from him.

"We don't know anything else. Dwight is bringing her here for questioning. She didn't resist when he and Jamie arrived to arrest her. I wanted to tell you before someone in town spotted her and passed the word along to you. I didn't want you doing anything rash."

"What did you think I would do?" Ryker asked.

"I don't know. But in your shoes I would be pretty upset. Better to have you here. As soon as we know anything about Charlotte's whereabouts, I promise you will, too."

"Thanks for that."

Somewhere down the hall, a door opened and voices rose. Ryker turned toward the sound. "I want to see her," he said.

"Not until after we've questioned her."

Ryker knew this was the proper way to do things, and the best way to ensure that Kim's eventual prosecution stood up in court. But the idea of having to wait to find out where his daughter was ate at him. "I'll send someone in to wait with you," Gage said, and left the room.

Ryker paced. Gage had been so insistent that he come to the sheriff's department right away that he hadn't changed clothes. He was wearing jeans and a T-shirt, the clothing emphasizing his role here as just another civilian.

The door to the interview room opened and Jamie Douglas entered. The department's sole female deputy, Jamie was a tall, slender brunette with a reputation as a tough, smart cop. Like Ryker, she had grown up in Eagle Mountain. She was a few years older than Ryker, but he remembered her from school. "Hello, Ryker," she said. "Do you want a cup of coffee or anything?"

"No thanks. I'm wired enough without the caffeine."

Jamie sat, but he continued to pace. "Did you draw the short straw, having to babysit me?" he asked. "What does Gage think I'm going to do—run in there and attack Kim? He should know me better than that."

"I'm here to keep you company while you wait." She leaned back in the chair, deliberately casual. "We can talk about whatever you like, though I thought maybe you'd want to hear what happened when we arrested Kim."

He stopped, then dropped into the chair across from her. "Tell me," he said.

"We met the Jeep at the turnoff onto the county road," she said. "The driver pulled over and we asked him and

Kim to step out of the car. They both climbed out. Kim held up her hands and stood there, not resisting. She looked like she'd had a hard time of it, frankly."

"What do you mean?"

"Her clothes were filthy, she had scratches on her arms and her hair was a mess. I asked her about the scratches and she said Mick had pushed her out of the car and driven off."

"Where was Charlotte?"

"Kim said Charlotte was with Mick. She said she had run after the car, trying to get to Charlotte, but Mick just sped up. She fell, chasing him, and that was how she got so dirty and scratched up."

"Why did he throw her out of the car?"

"She said it was because she wanted to take Charlotte back to you. That made Mick mad, so he left her out there in the middle of nowhere. She said he had done it before— left her alone with nothing to punish her—but he always came back, usually after a few minutes, or sometimes after a few hours. She said she thought she had been there two hours or more when she saw the Jeep driver and decided to flag him down and ask for help."

"Where are Mick and Charlotte now?" Ryker said. That was the only question that really mattered.

"She said she doesn't know. They knew their tent was being watched, so they couldn't go back there. She had wanted to drop Charlotte off in town and leave with Mick, but he refused."

"Why would he refuse?" Ryker asked. "It's not like he was ever interested in Charlotte before. I always thought he was the main reason Kim stayed away."

"She didn't say. After we got her in the cruiser and gave her some water she didn't say much of anything at all, except to insist that she doesn't know where Mick or Charlotte are right now."

"They must have been staying somewhere since they left their camp," Ryker said.

"I asked her if there was somewhere we could take her, to pick up the rest of her belongings," Jamie said. "I was hoping that might lead us to Charlotte. But Kim just said no. And after that, she clammed up."

He rubbed the back of his neck. "Why did she take Charlotte in the first place?"

"Gage and Travis will find out as much as they can," Jamie said.

"What about the feds? Are they on their way to question her?" Once the FBI arrived, Kim would be even further out of his reach.

"I don't think they've been notified yet."

"They'll be involved sooner rather than later," Ryker said.

"Declan and Shane are driving all the Jeep roads near where we picked up Kim, looking for any sign of the white Jeep or any kind of encampment," she said. "They'll stop anyone they see and ask about Mick and Charlotte."

Maybe they would get lucky and find their new hiding place, but Ryker wasn't one to count on luck. "Did Gage find out anything more about Mick Davis?" he asked.

"I don't know," Jamie said. "He didn't mention it."

He probably wouldn't have said anything to Jamie if he had, Ryker thought. He got up and began to pace again. Jamie pulled out her phone and began scrolling. Somewhere in the distance a phone rang. A door opened and closed. Muffled voices swelled, then faded, the words indistinguishable.

The door to the interview room opened and Dwight Prentice stuck his head in. The lanky blond, thirty-four years old, had been with the department longer than anyone except Travis and Gage. "Ryker, could you come with me?"

Ryker followed him into the hallway. "Kim asked to talk to you," Dwight said.

"Good." He had a lot of things he wanted to say to her, but he reminded himself the most important thing right now was to listen.

"Are you armed?" Dwight asked him.

"No." He had been in such a hurry to get here, he hadn't taken his gun out of the safe he kept it in at home.

Dwight looked pained. "You know I have to check."

"I know." He held out his arms and allowed Dwight to frisk him. He was furious with Kim, but he would never have tried to kill her. But his fellow deputies had to always assume the worst in order to prevent tragedy.

He followed Dwight down the hall to another interview room. Gage opened the door for them, and the sheriff looked up from the table, where he sat across from Kim.

Jamie had been right—she looked rough. She had muddy smears down her cheeks and her eyes were red-rimmed, as if she had been crying. Her hair was a snarled nest, and one knee of her jeans was ripped, and not in a fashionably deliberate way. "Oh, Ryker, I'm so sorry," she moaned, and put her head down on the table and began to sob.

Travis stood. "You can sit here," he said.

Ryker took the seat and looked across at his ex-wife as she continued to sob. Most of the heat of his anger had dissipated. She was such a pathetic figure, not worth the energy it would take to muster any hatred.

Long minutes passed, her sobs the only sound in the room. Dwight hadn't come in, leaving Travis, Gage and Ryker to watch her. After a while, the sobs subsided, and she raised her head. She didn't say anything, so Ryker asked, "Where is Charlotte?"

"I don't know." Her voice sounded scratchy and raw. "If I did, I promise I would tell you."

"Where do you think she is?"

"I don't know that either!" Her voice rose on the last word, into a wail. Travis rested his hand on Ryker's shoulder, whether to steady him or because he feared Ryker might lunge across the table and throttle her, he didn't know. The sheriff needn't have worried about physical violence. Ryker wasn't going to lay a hand on Kim. She wasn't worth the effort. "Why did you take her?" he asked.

"Because I'm her mother. Mick agreed it was time. He had found this mining claim we were going to live on, off-grid. Charlotte was going to live with us. That was the plan all along. I told you when I left."

"I never agreed to the plan," he said.

"But I'm her mother." She sat up straighter, shoulders squared, and glared at him. This show of indignation might have been comical under other circumstances.

He wasn't going to waste time arguing the point. "Is she all right?" he asked.

"She's fine. She's having a wonderful time."

"You stole her away from her home. You took her from her family and friends. How could she be happy?" So much for his attempt to remain unemotional.

"Mick and I are her family, too. She was having fun with us."

"Mick isn't related to her. What is he going to do to her?" He had to force the words out, all the terrible possibilities behind them closing his throat.

She slumped. Ryker stared at her, frustration warring with fatigue. "Why did you want to talk to me?" he asked finally.

"I don't want you to think I'm a bad person," she said. "I wanted to tell you I'm sorry. I was trying to do the right thing and bring her back to you when Mick threw me out."

"Why did you change your mind about keeping her?"

"It's not that I didn't want her anymore, it's just that we weren't quite ready to have her with us. I guess I got a little overexcited and jumped the gun. Mick said he had a place for us to live, but it was just a shack and a tent. Not really the kind of place to bring a kid."

"Where was that?" he asked.

"I already told the sheriff about it. But we didn't stay there long. Mick decided we needed somewhere a little farther off the beaten path. But then we only had the tent, and I never realized it gets so cold in the mountains at night, you know?"

"You should have called me. I would have come to get her."

"I couldn't do that. I mean, you're a cop. Mick didn't like that. So I told him we could just drop her off in town and someone would make sure she got back to you."

This was a child she was talking about, not a package to be left at lost and found. But he reined in his anger. "Why didn't you do that?"

"Mick didn't want to do that. We argued and that's when he ended up leaving me by the side of the road. I was sure he would calm down and come back soon, but he didn't. And I was getting awfully thirsty out there, so I flagged down a guy for help. Only he had to go and call 911." She let out a long sigh. "But I guess it's for the best."

"It's not for the best if Charlotte isn't home safe," Ryker said.

"You think I'm an awful person and I'm not!" She began to cry again, but her tears didn't move him.

"Where are Mick and Charlotte now?" he demanded.

"I don't know." She buried her face in her hands.

He kept his fists clenched at his sides, wanting to shake her. "Where did you stay last night?"

"We slept in the Jeep. This morning he said he had found a new place for us to stay, but he didn't say where. But you don't need to worry. I'm sure he'll take good care of her."

"She belongs with me. You never should have taken her."

"Why are you being so mean to me?" she wailed.

He looked over at Gage. "I've had enough."

Gage opened the door and Dwight entered. "You need to come with us now," Dwight said, and took Kim's arm.

Her eyes widened in alarm. "Where are you taking me?"

"Downstairs, to the booking room and the holding cells," Dwight said. "You'll stay there until we can arrange transport to Junction."

"But you can't arrest me. I haven't done anything wrong."

"We've already told you you're charged with the kidnapping of Charlotte Vernon," Travis said. "We have you on tape saying that you understand the charges and your rights. I can read them to you again if you like."

"But I cooperated with you," she said. "I answered all your questions. And you can't charge me with kidnapping my own daughter."

"You don't have custody," Ryker said. "You haven't even seen Charlotte in three years."

"I'm still her mother."

"You need to come with me," Dwight said. "Stand up now."

She stood, but she looked furious. "I want a lawyer," she said.

"You have that right," Travis said. "We'll make the arrangements as soon as you're booked."

Dwight and Gage led her away, leaving Travis and Ryker alone. He felt utterly drained. "Did she tell you any more than she told me?" Ryker asked.

"No."

"What's this about a mining claim they were going to live on? Did Mick buy a place?"

"It doesn't sound like it," Travis said. "I think he had the idea that if they squatted there long enough, they could assume ownership. Or maybe he thought nobody would know, or he could scam someone into letting them stay. How did Kim seem to you?"

"What do you mean?"

"Is she how you remembered her?"

He tried to think back to the woman he had married. The one who had charmed him and made him believe they could make a life together. "I didn't marry her because I was in love with her," he said. "She was pregnant and I believed the baby was mine and I wanted to be there for her and the baby. She was pretty and outgoing and fun to be with, so I thought we could make it work. She was always a little…erratic. Very enthusiastic about one thing, then she would drop that and move on to something else. But once she met up with Mick…" He shrugged. "She became enthralled with him, and that doesn't seem to have changed."

"I can't decide if she's really that much under his control or if she's faking it," Travis said.

"I think she's that much under his control," Ryker said. "For what it's worth, I always thought he was behind her abandoning Charlotte. I wasn't happy about the two of them getting together, but I never thought she would turn her back on her baby. She was a good mother before she left with him." That knowledge was one thing that had kept him from losing it entirely after Charlotte disappeared. For all her faults, Kim had taken good care of Charlotte before she left, and he had held on to the hope that those motherly instincts still flourished inside her.

Gage returned to the room. "She's quieted down now," he said.

"Did you find out anything about Mick Davis?" Ryker asked. "Any reason the FBI might be worried about him?"

Gage looked past Ryker to the sheriff. "Davis has never been convicted of any offense related to children," Travis said.

"But?" Ryker asked.

"But he was questioned about the disappearance of a little girl in Gilcrest last year, where he and Kim were living at the time," Travis said. "A witness reported a man who fit his description seen with the girl about the time she disappeared. Nothing came of it. He was questioned and released."

Ryker's mouth was dry. "What happened to the little girl?" he asked.

"She's never been found."

"It may not mean anything," Gage said. "You know how these things work. Law enforcement questions a lot of people who turn out not to be related to the crime."

Right. Ryker had been one of them. But it didn't mean Mick wasn't involved in whatever happened with that little girl, or that he would take good care of Charlotte.

"We're putting everything into looking for him and Charlotte," Travis said. "We're sending up a helicopter as soon as it can get here from Delta. I'm asking every off-duty and reserve deputy to help. No one has said no."

"I can help." Ryker stood.

"You know that's not a good idea," Travis said.

If Ryker had been in Travis's shoes, he would have said the same thing. Law enforcement couldn't risk an enraged or distraught father confronting Mick and sending the situation spiraling out of control.

"I know it's hard," Gage said. "You need to find something else to focus on while we're doing our jobs. Did you see anything in the file I sent over?"

Ryker took a deep breath, and pulled his attention to Aiden's file. "Do you remember that handyman, Gary Langley?"

"What about him?" Travis asked.

Ryker explained about the man who had approached him the evening of the day Charlotte disappeared, and about Margery Kenner's mention of him in her statement. "The file states Langley told the sheriff's deputies that he sold the truck, but I couldn't find anything showing anyone followed up on the sale of his truck. Did he really sell it before Aiden disappeared, or did he get rid of it afterward?"

"He lives on a few acres east of town," Gage said. "I think he inherited the property from his family. He's been on disability for years."

"He said he had an accident at work the year after Aiden went missing," Ryker said. "I thought that was odd—he kept mentioning Aiden. Why didn't they look at him more closely at the time of Aiden's disappearance?"

"I'm not excusing them, but it was a small department, with few resources and not much experience," Travis said. "If I remember right, they followed up with him about the truck, he said he had sold it, and that's as far as it went."

"And they had already decided that I was the one who killed Aiden," Ryker said.

Travis nodded.

"Wasn't Langley related to one of the deputies back then?" Gage asked. "Married to his sister, or something?"

"Maybe so," Travis said. "He doesn't have a criminal

record that I'm aware of, but I promise I'll look at him a little more closely. Though it may not be right away."

"I understand," Ryker said. He didn't want anything distracting from the search for Charlotte. "But when you get a chance. It would be good to have some closure for Aiden's parents."

"In the meantime, go home and try to stay positive," Gage said. "You have to trust us. We've got your back."

But none of them were Charlotte's father. No matter how much they cared, he would always care more. No matter how much they fought, he would fight harder.

He left the sheriff's department but he didn't drive home. Instead, he headed east out of town, to the address he pulled up for Gary Langley. The property was a flat, scrubby acreage dotted with sagebrush. The house, a square wooden structure with flaking white paint and a metal roof streaked with orange rust, sat atop a small rise, a white van parked out front.

Ryker stopped his truck behind the van and sat for a moment studying the house. No dog barked and everything was so still he might have thought the property was unoccupied, except he saw the blinds move. A few moments later the door opened and Langley, leaning on a thick wooden cane, stepped out.

Ryker got out of his truck and walked up to meet Langley on the porch. "Deputy." Langley tipped his head in acknowledgment. "What can I do for you?"

"We talked that first day my daughter went missing," Ryker said. "I'm sorry I didn't remember you then. I was still in shock, I guess. But later, I remembered. You used to drive a red pickup, didn't you? For your handyman business?"

"I did. But why would you remember that?"

"I was a nineteen-year-old gearhead. I paid attention to

cars and trucks. I really liked yours. That red color—whatever happened to it?"

"I sold it. It looked nice, but I wanted something that would hold more tools. I ended up buying a van. I still have it." He nodded toward the battered white van in the driveway. "I had it converted to hand controls to make it easier for me to drive."

"I guess it was foolish of me to hope you still had it." Ryker attempted to look sheepish. "Who did you sell it to?"

"A fellow from Texas. But that was years ago. He probably got rid of it a long time ago."

"You never know. You don't remember his name, do you?"

"No, I don't." Langley scowled, the expression almost lost in the deep folds of wrinkles and jowls.

"What year did you sell it to him?"

"I don't remember. A long time ago."

"But you still had it when Aiden went missing."

"No, I sold it before then."

Ryker nodded. "Someone told me they thought you still had it then. They saw you driving it—probably helping search for Aiden."

"They were wrong." Langley shifted, the cane thumping hard on the porch floor. "Don't you have better things to do than to worry about an old truck? Shouldn't you be out searching for your daughter?"

"You're right. I'm just trying to stay busy while I wait for the sheriff's department to coordinate the search. Since I'm Charlotte's dad, they don't want me too directly involved. I won't bother you anymore. Thanks again for all your help."

He left, never completely turning his back on the older man. As he slid into his truck he glanced toward the porch. Langley was still there, glowering at him. He had made it a point to mention his disability again. Was that merely a habit, or did he want to emphasize how incapable he was of doing anything harmful? Maybe he was now. But when Aiden was alive, Langley had been a hardy, strong man. Ryker remembered something about him coaching youth soccer. He might even have known Aiden.

He started the truck and backed out of the driveway. Maybe Langley had nothing to do with Aiden's disappearance, but someone should have checked. Instead of deciding Ryker was guilty and focusing only on him, someone should have done a better job of searching for Aiden's killer. It might be too late to find whoever was responsible now. But that didn't mean it wasn't worth trying.

Chapter Thirteen

Harper was back at search and rescue headquarters Thursday evening for regular training. Attendance at these sessions was mandatory for rookies like her, and most of the veterans attended as well, if they were able. "Jake isn't here tonight because everyone at the sheriff's department is putting in overtime to look for Charlotte Vernon," Hannah shared when they were all settled in an assortment of folding chairs and cast-off sofas in the concrete-floored main space of headquarters.

"Where are they searching?" Harper sat on the edge of her chair. "Has there been a new sighting?"

"I don't know," Hannah said. "But he asked us to all be ready to go out again if we're needed."

"We could help now." Anna rested one hand on the head of her search dog, Jacquie. The black standard poodle stood by her side, ears pricked at the word *search*.

"They're not ready for us yet," Danny said. "But they could need us later. So have your gear ready to go. For now, let's focus on reviewing best practices for transferring an injured person into a litter."

Harper tried to keep her mind on the instructions for moving a person from a vehicle to a litter, or from the ground to a litter. Depending on the patient's condition, they had to be stabilized, fitted with safety gear, and moved in a way that wouldn't worsen any injuries. She studied the slides Danny projected onto the wall, and made notes to review at home, but all the while her mind was on Charlotte and Ryker. Was he out with the search crews now, or had the sheriff insisted he remain home, waiting? Either way, how agonizing it must be for him. Charlotte had been gone a week with people who were strangers to her, even if one of them was her mother.

"Let's take a break, then we'll come back and practice some of these transfer techniques." Danny shut down the slideshow and people began to stand and stretch. Harper moved into a back hallway and called Ryker. The phone rang five times before going to voicemail. "Hey, I'm at a search and rescue meeting and heard the sheriff's department has everyone out searching for Charlotte. I hope this means they're close to finding her. Call me when you get a chance." She ended the call, then sent a text with the same message.

"Something wrong?" She looked up to find Hannah standing in front of the door to the ladies' room.

"I was just trying to call Ryker to see if he knew what was going on with the search for Charlotte." She slid her phone into the pocket of her jeans.

"Jake didn't tell me much," Hannah said. "I never know if that's because he doesn't know any more, or if he's keeping sheriff's department business confidential. Probably a little of both."

"Something must have happened, to send them back out on the search," Harper said.

"I think you're right," Hannah said. "I just don't know what that is." She put her arm around Harper. "Waiting and not knowing is awful. I was really glad for this meeting tonight to distract myself."

RYKER STUDIED THE map of the mining district spread out on his bed. On it, he had circled the Ida B Mine, where Harper had found Charlotte's hair ribbon. Though Kim hadn't been sure of the name of the place, he believed this was the claim Mick had intended to squat on. He had also circled the place where he and Harper had found the abandoned camp. Finally, he had drawn a red *X* at the intersection where deputies had arrested Kim. The three sites were all within a five-mile radius in the Galloway Basin Mining District. Though it was possible Mick might have decided to move on after abandoning Kim, Ryker was betting that he had found a new hiding place within the district.

The sheriff had probably studied a similar map and come to the same conclusion, but Gage had checked in when they shut down the search due to darkness to report they had found nothing. They planned to resume their efforts in the morning and focus on the eastern half of the district, a network of narrow roads pockmarked with small mining claims.

Those were also the roads most frequented by tourists, who hiked among the mining ruins photographing the rusting equipment and falling-down shacks, or searched among the debris for iron spikes, hand-cast nails and other souvenirs of the past—even though signs pleaded with people to leave all artifacts in place.

Even though these sites were most likely to offer habitable buildings, Ryker reasoned that Mick would avoid crowds and head to more remote locations. That meant the west side of the district, with its steeper, less-used roads and fewer abandoned mines. He used a highlighter to trace a route into this area, then folded the map and tucked it into the side of his pack. He had food and water, rain gear and first aid supplies. He was prepared to spend the night out if he had to, but he had purposely packed light. If he found Charlotte, he would need to carry her as well as the pack.

Maybe he was wasting his time. Mick could be two states away by now. Charlotte's Amber Alert was still active, and the sheriff would have updated the bulletin with the information that she was traveling with a lone male. If they got lucky, someone else would spot the pair and contact law enforcement.

But Ryker had to do something. He couldn't sit at home waiting any longer.

His headlights cut a narrow path up the rocky road leading to his first destination, a long-abandoned operation designated on the map as the Lucky Six Mine. Ryker drove as far as the trailhead for a popular hike up Jack's Peak and parked. From this point the road grew much rougher, with sharp, narrow turns and steep drop-offs. He would need better light to navigate it safely.

He rolled down the window and shut off the engine. Silence wrapped around him, the darkness so complete it was as if someone had thrown a blanket over him. Gradually, he was able to make out the shadowed outlines of rocks and scrubby trees beyond the parking area, and some of the tension in his chest released. He breathed in deeply, taking in the scent of dust and piñon.

A high wail rose in the distance, jolting him to attention and standing the hairs along his arms on end. A series of yips descended the scale and he recognized the song of a group of coyotes. They sounded very close, though he knew sound carried far in the clear air, echoing off rocks, so that it was hard to tell from which direction the noise originated.

Could Charlotte hear these same noises? Was she frightened by them? He tried to remember if they had heard coyotes before. He wished now he had taken her camping so that the night sounds of the wilderness were more familiar to her, and not frightening.

When Charlotte had first disappeared, he had comforted himself with the thought that she would be all right with Kim. For all her faults, she had been a good mother in Charlotte's early years. Now he didn't even have that solace. Charlotte was alone with a man who had been a suspect in the disappearance of another little girl. Maybe he had nothing to do with that crime, but what if he had?

He pushed the thought away. He wouldn't be able to function if he started playing that awful *what if* game. He needed to stay focused on Charlotte—on finding her and getting her to safety. To do that, he needed to sleep, and be ready to hike hard at first light.

HARPER SET HER alarm for 3:00 a.m. She slipped out of bed as quietly as possible, then dressed and collected the pack she had filled the night before with food, water, extra clothing and first aid supplies. She left a note for her parents. *Gone to help search for Charlotte.* Then she tiptoed outside to her car and set off toward the mountains. On the way, she called her office and left a voicemail explaining she needed to take a personal day.

She passed no other cars this time of night, and once out of town, the darkness was complete. Stars glittered between the peaks of distant mountains, which were little more than gray smudges against the sky. She watched carefully for her first turnoff. She had memorized the directions to the Jack's Peak trail, but there were no road signs out here and if she missed a turn or mistakenly took the wrong road, she would be lost within minutes. GPS was useless on these backroads, and within minutes of leaving the highway she had no cell signal anyway. She gripped the steering wheel more tightly and stared out the windshield, praying she was doing the right thing.

The roads grew progressively rougher as she climbed in elevation. Deep ruts and protruding rocks forced her to proceed at a crawl, gritting her teeth as she navigated tight turns. Her Subaru wasn't exactly designed for this kind of terrain. After one particularly nerve-racking passage she was debating parking the car and hiking the rest of the way when her headlights illuminated the back of a truck.

She pushed the car a little faster, and soon was able to verify it was Ryker's truck. Triumph surged through her and she tapped her horn, intending to alert him to her arrival.

But he didn't appear. By the time she parked, she realized the truck was empty. She shut off the engine of her car and realized the sky was lighter, the outlines of rocks and trees and mountain peaks more distinct against a sky that was fast transforming from gray to lavender to pink.

She looked around, wondering which direction he had traveled. The trail ahead was the one she had taken on that long-ago hike, up to the top of Jack's Peak. That didn't seem a likely destination for a couple fleeing with a little girl. That left the road past this parking area. She walked over to study it more closely and grimaced. Calling it a road would be overstating the situation. Twin rocky tracks led across more rocks, some the size of footstools. No way would her car get down that safely. Ryker's truck, on the other hand, probably could have navigated the route. So why hadn't he taken it?

She returned to her car and shouldered her pack and started down the road. She hadn't gone far before she discovered the reason Ryker had not driven this way. A rockslide cascaded from a cliff on the right, burying the track hip-deep in stones and making it impassable. She studied the pile of rocks, looking for footprints, or any indication that Ryker had come this way.

She didn't find anything. Maybe she was wasting her time. Then again, she didn't have anything better to do today. She tightened the straps of her pack and began climbing.

She hiked for an hour after scaling the rockslide. The sun rose, warming the air, and she settled into a comfortable rhythm. She told herself she would go for another hour before she turned back. This was good training for rescue, even if she didn't find Ryker.

They had gone hiking once together in high school. What was the trail they had taken? Up on Dakota Ridge, she thought, a wooded trail in the fall, through showers of red and gold aspen leaves. It looked like something out of a romance movie, or at least it had felt like that to her, so young and so in love. They had stopped for a picnic lunch in a sheltered spot off the trail and ended up making love on that carpet of leaves, Ryker's coat spread beneath them. That might even have been the day their child was conceived.

She was walking head-down, lost in these memories, when a movement ahead startled her. Ryker stepped out from behind a boulder. "I thought someone was following me," he said. "Harper, what are you doing here?"

RYKER COULDN'T SAY he wasn't happy to see Harper, though acknowledging that felt selfish. Mick Davis was a convicted felon who might be dangerous. Having Harper here meant she might be at risk. So he didn't tell her how good it was to have her here. "You shouldn't be here," he said.

"Why not?" She met his gaze, unruffled. Stubborn. He remembered that same expression on her face when she had told him she was pregnant. Young as she was, she had been so certain she was making the right decision, so confident in her ability to see a tough thing through to the end. "I want to help, and two sets of eyes are better than one. Not to mention, it's safer to hike with a partner. And when we find Kim and her boyfriend, it will be the two of us against the two of them—better odds."

The sheriff must have done a good job of keeping the news about Kim quiet. "Kim isn't with Mick anymore," he said. "She was arrested and brought in yesterday afternoon. Charlotte is alone with Mick."

She looked exactly the way he had felt when he had heard the news—as if someone had punched her in the gut. She hugged her arms across her stomach and stared at him. "You don't think he'll hurt her, do you?"

"I don't know. All I know about the man is his criminal record, and that's more than enough to make me worried."

She straightened, visibly pulling herself together. "Where do you think they are?"

He looked up the road they were on. "I plotted all the points where they have been seen on a map. There's a mine at the end of this road that looked like a good place for him to hole up. Kim said they were looking for old mining claims with structures on them where they could live."

"How far is the mine from here?" she asked.

"A couple more miles, I think."

"It's a long way to walk with a little kid. And I didn't see any sign of the white Jeep, or any other vehicle, back at the trailhead."

"I'm wondering if he didn't drive up here before that slide blocked the road." He kicked at a rock in one of the ruts. "Even before the slide, the road was almost impassable, but the lack of traffic might have appealed to him. And he's shown a penchant for reckless driving." One more way he was endangering Charlotte.

"Then let's go." Harper set out walking. He caught up with her. "Where is Kim now?" she asked.

"I don't know. Probably on her way to jail in Junction."

"How did they manage to arrest her? Or are you allowed to say?"

"She said Mick kicked her out of the car and abandoned her on the side of the road. She flagged down a car and the driver called 911. She said it wasn't the first time Mick had left her somewhere like that, but he had always come back before."

"She must have been frantic, being separated from her daughter like that," Harper said.

"She seemed more upset about being arrested than worried about Charlotte." He tamped down his anger against Kim. He needed to focus on Charlotte, not his ex-wife. "She said Mick wouldn't hurt Charlotte, but I'm not so sure."

Harper moved over to link her arm with his. "You must be worried sick, but you're doing everything you can. And you're not the only one looking. Hannah said the sheriff has called in every available deputy to search for Charlotte, and search and rescue volunteers are on standby."

"I know. The sheriff sent me home to wait, but I couldn't sit idle and do nothing."

"Neither could I. That's why I came looking for you."

He looked down into her eyes and it was as if he was eighteen again. She had been the one person he had felt had truly understood him back then. Maybe things hadn't changed that much. "It helps, having you here," he said.

"Then I'm glad to be here." She squeezed his arm, then moved away again, picking up the pace.

They climbed a steeper section of the road and emerged

on a flat bench of land. A three-foot section of iron track jutted from a pile of rocks to their right, and the rusted shell of an ancient boiler crowned another pile of crumbling rocks, the bright ocher color identifying this as the waste rock left over from mining. Fifty feet beyond, the remains of a small shack leaned drunkenly to the left, its roof caved in, windows and door vacant holes in the weathered gray logs that remained. "Is this where Mick thought they could live?" Harper asked.

"I'm pretty sure this is the Lucky Six Mine," Ryker said. "This is the place I picked out on my map, though Kim swore she didn't know where Mick intended to go." He turned a slow circle, surveying the area. A few scrubby piñons dotted the mostly barren landscape. "The road ends here, so he would have had to park and walk if he wanted to go any farther."

Harper moved toward the shack. "I don't think anyone is living in here," she said as she peered into the open doorway. "It's full of broken boards and rusty metal roofing."

Ryker picked up a chunk of the mine waste and weighed it in his hand. "There are a couple of other places we can look, if you're up for it."

"Sure. Let me duck over behind those rocks and pee, then we can head back." She pointed to a pile of boulders at the edge of the bench.

"Okay." He turned his back on the boulders and looked up the hill, past the shack. He could just make out a narrow footpath that led up the hill and around another outcrop. Should they go a little farther and check out whatever was up there? But it didn't make sense that Mick would have come all this way on foot, especially with Charlotte in tow.

Then again, the man had been quick to ditch Kim, who had lived with him for three years. How long would it take before he decided a four-year-old was too much trouble? The thought of Charlotte left alone in the wilderness blurred his vision for a moment.

A shout from Harper brought him back to himself. He spun around in time to see her run out from behind the boulders. "Come look at this!" she shouted, and motioned for him to join her.

He jogged over to her. She grabbed his hand and pulled him behind the boulders. There, wedged between the rocks and a stout piñon, was a dirty white Jeep.

Chapter Fourteen

Harper stared at the abandoned Jeep, throat tight. "They were here," she said, almost whispering, as if Mick Davis might be close enough to hear her.

"They're still here somewhere." Ryker moved toward the Jeep, then stopped and shifted his pack until he could extract a pair of nitrile gloves from it. "I'm going to take a look inside."

She moved in close behind him, careful not to touch anything, but wanting to see what he found. The smell of cigarette smoke and stale food hit them as soon as Ryker opened the front passenger door. Over his shoulder, she studied the worn black upholstery and dusty floor mats almost obscured by piles of food wrappers, crushed soft drink cans, empty plastic water bottles and cigarette butts. "He didn't leave the keys," Ryker noted. He peered under the seat. "Nothing here but more trash."

He moved to open the rear passenger door. Harper couldn't see as well into this space. "More trash," Ryker said. "Wait a minute." He leaned in and emerged seconds later holding something small and white. Harper's throat closed again as she recognized a child's sock—white with pink rosebuds at the cuff.

Ryker stared at the sock, and she wondered what he was

thinking. Was he angry? Afraid? Sad? Probably all of the above. "If they're here, we'll find them," she said. "I could hike back down until I get a cell signal and call for help."

He hesitated, frowning, then shook his head. "I don't like the idea of you heading out by yourself with Mick possibly nearby. He's probably armed."

"I don't like the idea of leaving you up here alone, either," she said.

"We'll look around together," he said. "If we see anything, we'll both go back and get help." He closed both vehicle doors, easing them shut so that they scarcely made a sound. Then he moved around to the driver's door, opened it, leaned in and released the hood. He moved around to the front of the vehicle, reached in and yanked out a tangle of wires. "That will slow him down if he comes back." He eased the hood down until it closed with a soft click.

Harper scanned the area around them. Silence closed in—the silence of a long-deserted area. "Where do you think they are?" she asked.

"There's a trail just past that old building," he said. "Let's see what's up there."

Tension vibrating through her, she followed him up a narrow, rocky path that scarcely passed for a trail. She fought to keep her balance as loose rocks rolled beneath her feet. If she was having this hard a time making it up here, what would it have been like for Charlotte? Had Mick carried her? That is, if they were even up here. She couldn't see any sign that anyone else had come this way, but how would she know? Footprints didn't show in the dry, rocky soil.

Ryker stopped and put out a hand to halt her. "I see some buildings up ahead," he said.

She moved up beside him, and put her hand on his back to steady herself. She peered in the direction he indicated and could just make out the side of a log cabin, and one section of its rusty metal roof. "We need to get off this trail." Ryker spoke with his mouth close to her ear, his voice soft, sending a shiver down her spine. "Mick might be watching for someone to come up this way."

She nodded, then followed as he moved off the trail and began picking his way on an indirect route toward the log building. He kept below the ridge as they hiked in a wide arc, then began to climb once more. At the top of the ridge they emerged behind what proved to be a trio of log cabins.

These buildings were in better shape than the one nearest the parking area. One had a roof that looked intact, and though none of them had real windows, the walls were upright, if unchinked, and two of them had doors. Harper sniffed the air. "I smell woodsmoke," she whispered. There was no sign of smoke near any of the cabins now but perhaps last night, when temperatures would have dropped, someone had lit a fire to cook dinner and keep warm.

"Stay here," Ryker said. "I'm going to try to get closer."

She shook her head. "We need to stay together."

He scowled, but rather than argue, he turned and started toward the nearest cabin, the one with the intact roof and a door. She followed, moving as quietly as possible, every nerve tense, ears straining for the sound of anyone nearby. They reached the rear of the cabin and pressed their backs against the rough wood. Then Ryker inched toward the window opening, the rough wooden frame empty of glass. She darted past him to take up a position on the other side so she could look inside also.

It took a moment for her eyes to adjust to the dim interior. The floor was dirt, streaked with thin bars of sunlight showing through the gaps between the unchinked logs. At first, it appeared empty, then she focused on what appeared to be a heap of sleeping bags and blankets in the far corner. She reached out and gripped Ryker's arm. "They were here!" she whispered.

He nodded, and leaned in to examine the space more thoroughly. The air smelled of old wood and dust, and the stronger aroma of wet ash from an extinguished fire, though she couldn't see signs of any blaze within that one bare room. Perhaps they had lit a campfire outside, to the front of the cabin.

Ryker tapped her arm and indicated they should move on. She started to turn away, but as she did so, something moved over by the blankets. She grabbed Ryker's hand and pulled him back, then pointed into the cabin. As they stared, the blankets definitely shifted. She caught a glimpse of a small hand, and a flash of blond hair.

Ryker vaulted over the windowsill and raced to the pile of blankets. "Charlotte," he called, and pulled back the blankets. "Charlotte, honey, are you all right?"

The child blinked up at him, then reached up with her arms. "Daddy!" she called, and Ryker scooped her up, blankets and all.

Harper blinked back tears as she witnessed this reunion. "It's okay, sweetheart," Ryker said, smoothing back Charlotte's hair. "You're safe with me now. I'm going to take you home." He moved toward the door, but before he reached it, it burst open.

A wiry man with short blond hair and a scruffy beard filled the doorway. He hefted an axe in one hand. "Put her down," he ordered. "Do it now or I'll kill you."

RYKER HADN'T SEEN Mick Davis in years but he had no doubt the blond threatening him now was the man Kim had left him for. Charlotte began to sob, and Ryker tightened one arm around her and took a step back, toward the window. He kept his gaze on Mick and that axe, and debated whether or not he could draw his gun from beneath his jacket without putting his daughter in danger.

The light streaming through the window shifted. He didn't look over, but hoped Harper was retreating out of harm's way. Mick gave no sign he had noticed, his gaze remaining fixed on Ryker and Charlotte. Time to end this stare-down. "I'm going to take my daughter and leave," Ryker said.

Mick took a firmer grip on the axe. "And I told you to put her down."

Ryker could feel the weight of the gun at his back, but he couldn't risk Charlotte. She shifted against him and made a whimpering sound, and he cradled her head in his hand, wanting to comfort her and needing to protect her. To get her to safety. "What do you want with her, Mick?" he asked. "She'll just slow you down when you try to get away."

"She's my little insurance policy. To get to me, they risk hurting her and no one wants that, do they?" He hefted the axe higher and took a step toward them.

Charlotte wailed, and the light shifted again as Harper moved into the doorway behind Mick. She clutched a rusty iron bar in both hands. Before Ryker had time to react, she brought the bar down hard on the back of Mick's head.

He toppled like a felled tree, the axe trapped beneath him. He groaned, and tried to push himself up on hands and knees. Ryker kicked him hard in the chest and he crumpled again, then Ryker raced past him out the door. Harper stood, both arms wrapped around herself, looking shaken.

"We need to get out of here," Ryker said.

She nodded, but continued to stare past him at Mick.

Ryker looked back over his shoulder and watched Mick

rock up on all fours, groaning. Then he turned back to Harper. "Come on." He touched her shoulder.

He jogged away from the cabin, relieved to hear her right behind him. When they were a hundred yards or so from the cabins he paused to get his bearings. They needed to work their way off this ridge, back toward the trail that eventually led to the parking area and his truck. A shouted curse from Mick jolted him to action once more. He whirled to momentarily face the cabins—and Mick. The other man shouldn't be standing after the blow Harper had given him, but somehow he was on his feet and staggering after them. But he wouldn't be able to run. All he and Harper had to do was put more distance between themselves and Mick and hike the two miles to his car. Not the easiest thing he had ever done, but not impossible, either.

A whistling sound cut the air, and air rushed past his left shoulder, followed by the sharp report of gunfire. "He's shooting at us!" Harper cried.

Ryker bent over, shielding Charlotte with his body. "Run for cover!" he shouted.

HARPER DARTED INTO a clump of trees at the very edge of the clearing. She huddled behind the gnarled trunk of a juniper, the silvery bark peeling away like flowing hair. Was the trunk stout enough to stop a bullet? She peeked between the trees, looking back toward the cabins. Mick Davis, blood matting his hair and staining one side of his face and beard, held a large pistol and stalked toward them.

Ryker crashed through the trees to join her. He dropped to his knees behind her and shoved Charlotte toward her. "Charlotte, you remember Harper, don't you?" he said. "She's going to take care of you for a minute, but I'll be right here."

Harper gathered the girl close. "Hello, Charlotte," she said, and forced a smile. She moved farther into the cover of trees. Charlotte stared at her with wide, frightened eyes, but didn't say anything. Ryker pulled a gun from beneath his jacket at his back and moved to steady himself behind the juniper's wide trunk.

Harper startled at the first shot, even though she had known it was coming. Charlotte covered both ears with her hands and squeezed her eyes shut. Her trembling vibrated through Harper, who pulled her close and spoke in her ear, in what she hoped was a soothing tone. "It's going to be okay," she said. "Your dad is going to take care of us."

"He's back in the cabin." Ryker duckwalked to them. "We need to move. Can you carry her for a little bit, in case I have to return fire again?"

She shuddered at the idea of more bullets flying, but nodded. "Of course."

He helped her stand, and she settled Charlotte more comfortably on her hip. The child was heavy, but not any heavier than the full packs she had carried on search and rescue missions. "We're ready," she said.

Ryker led the way, not back to the path, but threading through the trees and rocky uplift. They had to move slowly, picking their way around obstacles, but no more bullets whistled past them, and she didn't hear anyone pursuing them. They were traveling downhill, and she reasoned that Ryker was taking them on a route that would eventually meet the road they had come in on. They moved quickly, not speaking. After a while, he took Charlotte again. The little girl put her arms around his neck and laid her head on his shoulders, but didn't say a word.

Harper thought they had been walking forty-five minutes to an hour when Ryker abruptly stopped. "What is it?"

she asked, hurrying to stand beside him. Then she saw that the ground fell away in front of them.

"We're cliffed out," he said. "We'll have to backtrack."

Charlotte started to cry. Ryker shifted her to his other hip. "We're not going back to Mick," he said. "You're safe with me."

"Can we stop and rest a little?" Harper asked. "Maybe get something to eat and drink, and think about what we need to do next?" The sun was high in the sky now and her stomach grumbled.

"Good idea." He set Charlotte on her feet. "Do you need to use the bathroom, honey?" he asked.

She nodded. "I'll take you," Harper said. She offered her hand and Charlotte took it. The two picked their way over fallen tree limbs and scattered rocks to a sheltered spot in a thicket of shrubs. When they had both relieved themselves, Harper smoothed back Charlotte's hair and looked into her eyes. "How are you feeling?" she asked.

"Scared."

"I'm a little scared, too," Harper admitted. "But your dad and I are going to protect you and we're going to get you back home." She had a dozen questions she wanted to ask, about what exactly had happened to this child, but now wasn't the time to ask them. It wasn't even her place to ask them. She would need to leave that to Ryker. "We probably have a lot more walking to do to get to where your dad has parked his truck," she said instead. "Are you up for it?"

Charlotte bit her lower lip. "Can we eat something first?"

"Yes. Absolutely. Come on, let's get back to your dad."

Ryker had removed his pack and had some of the contents laid out on the ground—two water bottles, a half-dozen protein bars, two sandwiches and a couple of apples.

He looked up at their approach. "I've got ham and cheese," he said.

"I've got peanut butter and jelly." Harper removed her own pack. "And candy bars."

Charlotte looked livelier than she had all day. "Can I have a peanut butter and jelly sandwich?"

"Of course. And if you're still hungry after you eat it, we'll split a candy bar." She sat cross-legged on the ground and Charlotte copied the posture. Harper distributed the food and Ryker unwrapped his own sandwich. Then he cut up one of the apples and passed out slices. When she was done eating, Charlotte wiped her hands on her dress and looked at Ryker. "Do you know where Mama is?"

Ryker looked flummoxed by the question. "Your mom is safe," he said. "You do know she wasn't supposed to take you away from me like that, don't you?"

"I know."

Ryker didn't look any happier. Harper could almost see his calculating what to ask next. "Were you surprised to see your mom?" Harper asked.

Charlotte turned to her. "She said she was going to take me to get ice cream." She looked back to Ryker. "She said it was okay with you."

"It wasn't," Ryker said. "If she had come to me and asked, I would have arranged for all of us to visit together. I never tried to keep your mother from you, no matter what she might have told you."

"She said it was her turn to take care of me now. Her and Mick." She made a face, like she had eaten something sour.

"You don't like Mick," Harper guessed.

She nodded.

Ryker leaned toward her, rigid with tension. "Mick didn't hurt you, did he?"

Harper held her breath, waiting for the answer. Charlotte shrugged. "He didn't hit me—though he said he would if I didn't do what he said. He yelled a lot—at me and at Mama. I didn't like that. And I was really scared when he pushed her out of the car and kept me with him. I kept telling him I wanted to go home." She began to cry, and Ryker gathered her close, pulling her into his lap and rocking her.

He looked over her head and met Harper's gaze, and the pain in his eyes made her want to weep, too. She settled for moving closer and rubbing Charlotte's back. "It's okay," she said. "Your dad isn't going to let anything happen to you."

After a while, the little girl's breathing grew more even. Harper thought she had fallen asleep.

"Do you know where we are?" Harper asked Ryker.

He looked up at the sun high overhead in a sky the color of forget-me-nots. "If we keep heading east, we should hit the road," he said. "But we have to find a way down the ridge."

"What about Mick? Do you think he's still following us?"

"I don't know," he admitted. "But you hit him pretty hard. He's bound to have a concussion. I doubt he's moving all that quickly. And he doesn't really need Charlotte. If I was him, I'd take the chance to get away while I could."

"But you disabled his car."

"I did. I hope that will slow him down. All I really care about now is getting Charlotte home. The rest of the force can deal with Mick."

He put one arm around her. "I'm sorry you got dragged into this."

"I'm not," she said. "I don't like to think what would have happened if I hadn't sneaked up behind Mick and hit him." The sound of that metal bar striking his skull wouldn't leave her anytime soon. The moment had been awful, but not nearly as awful as it would have been seeing him use that axe against Ryker or Charlotte. "If he had a gun all that time, why did he threaten you with the axe?" she asked.

"I think he had probably gone to chop wood, so he had the axe in his hand at the time. I guess he thought it would be enough." He squeezed her shoulder. "I take back what I said before. I'm not sorry you're here. And not just because you went after Mick with that iron bar."

She leaned against him. Being here with him and Charlotte felt right. They were a good team. "We should get going," he said. "I want to get back to the truck before dark. The sooner we're away from Mick, the better I'll feel."

She nodded, and shoved herself to her feet. She wanted to be away from Mick, too, though she hated to end this moment with Ryker—just the two of them and Charlotte, without anyone else to interfere.

Chapter Fifteen

Friday morning, Deputy Jamie Douglas glanced at the woman next to her as they waited for the elevator that would take them to the basement-level holding cells. "Do you really think this will work?" she asked.

Adelaide Kinkaid, the sheriff's department's office manager, looked down at the cardboard tray containing two cups of coffee and a cinnamon roll. "I think it's worth a try. I'm good at getting people to confide in me. If they don't know me well, they assume I'm a harmless old woman."

She grinned and Jamie suppressed a laugh. Even though she was in her sixties, Adelaide never acted old, and she had a well-deserved reputation of knowing almost anything worth knowing about the goings-on in town, from the details of coming events to idle gossip. If anyone could get the information they needed, it would be her.

They rode the elevator down and passed through two sets of locked doors to the booking area and the two small holding cells, only one of which was occupied. Kim Vernon looked up at their approach. "It looks like you're going to be with us a little longer," Jamie said. "We're waiting for room to open up at the jail in Junction."

"I brought you some breakfast." Adelaide held up the tray. "And some company, if you're interested."

Kim stood and moved to the bars of the cell. "Who are you?"

"Adelaide Kinkaid. I'm a civilian who handles clerical work here at the station." She pulled a chair up to the bars and sat. "I heard about what happened to you and well, I've got a daughter about your age and a granddaughter Charlotte's age. I figure you must be beside yourself, being separated from her like this." She pushed the coffee cup through the opening of the bars. "I've got cream and sugar here if you want. And a cinnamon roll."

"Just cream, thanks." Kim accepted the little tub of cream and the roll, and settled on the end of the bunk, still eyeing the two women warily. Her intake sheet said she was twenty-nine, but she looked older, like someone who hadn't lived an easy life. What makeup she had put on at some point was mostly smeared off or collected in the creases around her eyes, and dark roots two inches long showed along the part of her hair. She was thin—almost bony— and dressed in a T-shirt and elastic-waist shorts.

"I have to stay here because Adelaide is a civilian," Jamie said. "But I feel for you. I've got a little girl, too. I just came back to work after my maternity leave and it's hard enough being away from her during my shift. I can't imagine being forced to leave her the way you were. And not knowing where she is."

Kim sipped coffee. "I'm sure Mick won't hurt her," she said. "He just has a bad temper, sometimes. And I forget myself and annoy him. He'll get over it. He always does."

"I couldn't help noticing the bruises on your arm." Adelaide nodded to the purpling patches showing below the sleeve of Kim's T-shirt. "Did Mick do that?"

Kim covered the bruises with her hand. "He would never lay a hand on Charlotte," she said. Jamie's stomach clenched as she read the doubt in the other woman's eyes. They really needed to find Charlotte, and if it took pretending to be friendly to the woman who had put her in danger in the first place, Jamie was willing to do it.

"Still, he isn't her real parent," Adelaide said. "You are. A little girl needs her mother."

"That's what I keep telling these cops." Kim sat up a little straighter. "They act like I'm some kind of criminal for wanting to take care of my little girl."

"Charlotte is such a beautiful child," Jamie said. That, at least, wasn't a lie.

Kim smiled. "She is. A lot of people say she favors me."

"Yes, I can see that," Adelaide said. "I know a lot of people are out looking for her. I hope they find her soon. I'm sure she really misses you."

"She was crying when Mick pushed me out of the Jeep," Kim said. She blinked rapidly, her eyes shiny.

"That wasn't right of him," Adelaide said. "Especially when all you wanted was to take care of your little girl."

"I know." Kim pinched a piece from the cinnamon roll, but didn't eat it.

"Where do you think he went?" Adelaide asked. "I mean, do you think he came back to try to find you after you got a ride from that guy in the Jeep? Or did he go back to your camp?"

"We were moving to a new place," Kim said. "But I don't know where we were going."

"He didn't even tell you that?" Adelaide looked disapproving. "Men. They don't really know how to communicate, do they?"

Kim laughed. "Isn't that the truth? I have to ask twenty questions to get anything out of Mick. It makes him so angry sometimes, but if he would just tell me what's going on in the first place it would save us all so much trouble."

"So he never said where this new camp was?" Adelaide asked.

Kim ate the piece of cinnamon roll and chewed thoroughly before she said, "Even if he had, I wouldn't have recognized the name. I'm not from around here."

"There are a lot of old mines up in that area," Adelaide said. "I haven't driven up there in a while, but I remember some of them even had buildings on them—little cabins that almost looked like you could move right in."

Kim nodded. "That's what we were looking for. Some place we could settle down and make a home. You know, live off-grid. We didn't want to bother anybody. We thought we had found a place, but after one night there we realized it was too close to popular Jeep roads. People were up there all the time. We couldn't have that. I mean, we were looking for peace and quiet, where we could get away from everybody."

"So I guess you decided to head farther into the mountains, away from the popular trails," Adelaide said.

"Exactly. Mick said he had found a new place on the map. It had three almost-complete cabins we could choose from. There was water nearby, and it was open, so we could add solar panels and maybe even have a little garden in the future. It sounded like just what we were looking for."

Jamie made a mental note of this. This could help narrow the search, even if Kim didn't come up with a name.

"You didn't worry about hikers interfering with you?" Adelaide asked. "People always want to poke around those old mine ruins."

"Mick had that all figured out," Kim said. "He said the road up to this place was really narrow and not used much, but after we got up there he would trigger a rockslide over the trail so no one could follow."

"Wouldn't that mean you would be trapped, too?" Jamie asked.

"He said he could drive over or around the rockslide. Most people wouldn't attempt it, but he could do it." Kim frowned. "He takes a lot of risks, driving. It scares me sometimes, but he always gets where he needs to go."

"That does sound like the ideal place to get away from it all," Adelaide said. "I wonder which mine that is."

"He may have said the name but I don't remember," Kim said. "Maybe something with a number in it?" She wrinkled her nose. "I'm not sure I have that right. I was trying to get Charlotte to eat her breakfast and I wasn't paying much attention. That was what set Mick off, actually. He didn't like me paying more attention to Charlotte than to him."

"Of course your daughter had to come first," Adelaide said.

"If they had more woman cops, maybe I wouldn't be in this cell," Kim said. "Men just don't understand."

Adelaide stood. "It was nice chatting with you. I'd better get to work now."

"I'll let you know when Junction is ready for your transfer," Jamie said.

Neither woman said anything until they were in the elevator again. "Do you think we can find that mine she was talking about?" Jamie asked.

"The sheriff has a map of the mining district with all the old claims marked on it," Adelaide said. "She gave us a pretty good description, with those three cabins and water nearby."

"Mick might not even have gone there," Jamie said.

"He might not. But this is the best lead I've heard of, so

it's definitely worth sending someone up there to check it out." Smiling, Adelaide led the way out of the elevator. She pulled out her phone and hit speed dial. "Sheriff? Jamie and I have been talking to Kim Vernon. She told us some things you need to hear."

GETTING BACK TO the road proved more difficult than Ryker had anticipated. Though he was sure they were traveling in the right direction, they repeatedly encountered obstacles that prevented them from moving in anything close to a straight line—a deep gully, an abrupt drop-off, or a soaring cliff face they weren't equipped to scale. Harper didn't say anything, but her silence and exhausted expression made him feel guilty once more for putting her through all of this.

Charlotte grew increasingly fussy. She didn't want to be carried, but when allowed to walk, would sit down and refuse to go any farther. She burst into tears more than once, and Ryker felt her frustration.

The sun was setting when Harper suggested they stop and make camp. "Walking around in the dark is too dangerous," she pointed out. "Better to build a campfire and settle in for the night. We'll do better if we start fresh in the morning."

By himself, Ryker probably would have pressed on, but one look at his daughter's tearstained face and Harper's sagging shoulders convinced him she was right.

Harper chose the campsite in an area sheltered by a large boulder on one side and a clump of brush on the other. "I took a class as part of my search and rescue training on how to build a makeshift camp," she said as she picked up fallen limbs and moved rocks to clear an area for them to settle in. "When we go out on a search or respond to assist someone injured in the wilderness, we might have to spend the night out." She slipped off her pack and removed two small packets. "These are emergency bivy bags," she said, turning the packet so that he could read the label, which showed a person inside a bright orange sleeping bag cinched around his body. "I only have two, but Charlotte will probably do better tucked up with one of us."

"What else do you have?" Charlotte knelt on the ground beside the pack and watched as Harper pulled out more items.

"I have a water filter, a first aid kit, a whistle and fire-starting materials." Harper laid these items out alongside her pack. Charlotte picked up the water filter and examined it. "Also a mirror that can be used to signal someone, an aluminum splint, another candy bar, some nuts, packets of drink mix, extra socks, a collapsible metal cup and a multi-tool."

Charlotte focused on the small pile of food. "I'm hungry," she announced.

"I still have one sandwich, one apple and a couple of protein bars in my pack," Ryker said. "And one of those space blanket things."

"Great," Harper said. "We should be able to get pretty comfortable. Let's start with a fire, then we'll pull together a picnic supper."

Charlotte pitched in to help collect tinder and smaller pieces of wood for their campfire. "I watched Mama and Mick build fires," she said, and dropped a handful of pine needles in the middle of the rock circle Harper had constructed as a fire ring.

Ryker soon had a fire going, and Harper spread the space blanket and the two bivy bags along one side of the fire. They sat on them and she divided their food, giving each of them a portion of sandwich, nuts, apple and candy.

"We'll save the protein bars for breakfast," she said. Then she mixed some of the powdered drink mix in the metal cup and passed it to Charlotte. "It's not a lot of food, but it's pretty well balanced, nutritionally."

Ryker bit off half his share of the candy bar and chewed.

"Daddy, you're not supposed to eat the candy first," Charlotte said. She was nibbling one corner of her quarter sandwich.

"I'm not too worried it's going to spoil my appetite," he said. He could have eaten three sandwiches after all the hiking he had done today.

Charlotte giggled. He hadn't meant to be funny, but hearing her sound so happy and normal lifted his spirits.

They finished eating and Charlotte settled beside Ryker. The light faded, sending them deeper and deeper in shadow, until he realized he could make out little beyond the circle of their fire. Charlotte lay down and was soon sleeping. He folded one side of the space blanket over her.

Harper moved closer. "Tomorrow we'll get to the road," she said. "And if we don't, maybe we'll see a plane. There's bound to be some aerial searches by now."

"I shouldn't have set out to find her on my own," he said. "I should have urged the sheriff to look here. If you hadn't been there to stop Mick…"

"Don't!" She clutched his arm. "You did what you did with the best of intentions. You wanted to find Charlotte. And it worked out. One night out here isn't going to hurt any of us."

He looked down at his sleeping daughter. She was curled on her side against him, breathing evenly. She was dirty, her clothes ragged and her hair tangled, but she didn't appear traumatized by what had happened. "I didn't want to leave Mick," he said. "But getting Charlotte to safety was more important."

"You disabled his car. He's not going to be able to get far."

"You're right. I guess I'm just a worrier." He blew out a breath. "Maybe it comes with being a cop. You know all the ways a situation can go bad."

"And you became a parent. I think that probably makes you worry more. Children are so vulnerable."

He turned to study her, the side of her face visible in the flickering light from the fire. "What happened with our baby?" he asked. "I never knew, exactly. That is, if you don't mind talking about it."

"I don't mind." She stared into the fire for a moment, then said, "I was six months pregnant. I felt huge and awkward, and really tired sometimes, but I was getting excited, too. My aunt, who I was living with, talked a lot about putting the baby up for adoption, but I didn't think I wanted to do that." She looked at him, then away. "I had this fantasy that I would have the baby, get back home to Eagle Mountain and find you, and you would insist that we be together. A real family. I didn't think my parents would be able to keep you away from your daughter, which meant they couldn't keep you away from me, either."

"I thought about getting on my motorcycle and going to Florida to look for you, but I worried you wouldn't be happy to see me. Maybe you agreed to leave because you believed I really had hurt Aiden."

"No!" She gripped his arm. "Leaving you was awful, but it was even worse because you were going through such a terrible thing alone."

"Not exactly alone. My parents stood by me, and there were other people." He covered her hand with his own. "But you were the one I wanted."

"My parents made me leave," she said. "My mom said we were going to see friends. She put me in the car and the next thing I knew, we were at the airport. I pitched such a fit, and I didn't calm down until my mom told me we were just going to Florida for a few days to see my aunt. She pitched it as a chance for me to get away and decide what I wanted to do with my life. It wasn't until the next day that I realized they weren't going to let me come home until after the baby was born. And they refused to let me get in touch with you. My aunt watched me like a jailer. She didn't let me have a phone or go online. After a while I just stopped trying. And after I lost the baby, I was too sad to come back. I was so angry with my parents, and I felt guilty and confused." She shook her head. "When I did finally get back to Eagle Mountain…"

"I wasn't here. It didn't seem worth hanging around without you here," he said. "And even after the sheriff said I wasn't a suspect in Aiden's death, there were still people who believed I must have been involved. Going somewhere else to school was a chance to make a fresh start. But I never forgot about you."

"I never forgot about you, either." She blew out a breath. "Anyway, I don't really know what happened with the baby. One day I was fine. The next day I felt really tired and kind of queasy, but I didn't think anything of it. I woke up in the middle of the night and I knew that something wasn't right. I was cramping and bleeding. I screamed for my aunt and it took her a while to calm me down. She took me to the hospital but before we even got there I knew it was too late. The doctor said I had miscarried. He didn't know why. He just said sometimes these things happen."

He slipped his arm around her shoulder and pulled her close. "I'm sorry," he said. "I used to think about you and the baby. I didn't know if it was a boy or girl. The idea of being someone's father was scary. But I liked it, too. I wanted the chance to do the right thing. To be a good dad."

"You're a good dad to Charlotte."

"I try. But it's hard not to make mistakes. And I worry about her not having a mother. My mom does her best, but it's not the same. I would never have intentionally kept Kim out of her life. If she had come to me and said she wanted visitation, or even shared custody, I would have tried to work something out. I want what's best for Charlotte. But now—now I could never trust Kim. And I don't want Mick having anything to do with my kid."

"Will Kim go to jail?" she asked.

"Probably. That's not for me to decide. I'll do my best to see that Mick serves time, for threatening us with that axe, and then shooting at us. And if I find out he laid a hand on Charlotte…" Anger closed his throat, so that he couldn't finish the sentence.

Harper rubbed his back, a soothing gesture. He became aware of the heat and pressure of her hand, and her soft curves pressed against his side. "Do you remember the time we hiked up on Dakota Ridge?" she asked.

Heat flooded him at the memory. "It's not the hiking I remember," he said.

She laughed, a throaty, sexy sound. "It felt so daring to sneak back into the woods like that and make love outdoors," she said. "So exciting."

"I was worried you'd think it was too risky," he said. "Or that you wouldn't be comfortable out in the open like that."

"I was a little nervous," she admitted. "But I was with you. That was all that really mattered." She turned her face to his and he kissed her, as if more than ten years hadn't passed since that afternoon in the woods. Her lips were as soft as he remembered, and she still felt just as tantalizing pressed against him. She shifted to face him, and slid her arms around his waist. He deepened the kiss, her mouth hot. Needy. Her breasts beneath his palms were fuller than they had been then, but his own response was as urgent as ever—that feeling of wanting so much, balanced on the edge of control.

A whimper beside them reminded him they were not alone. Harper pulled back. "Charlotte needs you," she said, and looked away.

He turned to his daughter. She was still sleeping, but more restless now, whimpering and tossing her head. He laid a hand on her side. "It's okay, honey," he said. "I'm right here."

Charlotte didn't open her eyes, but she settled. "Probably just a bad dream," Harper whispered.

He looked up and met her gaze, the reflection of the campfire sparking gold in her brown eyes. She smiled, a hint of regret in the expression. "We should try to get some sleep," she said. "We have a big day tomorrow."

She turned away and crawled into one of the bivy bags, then lay with her back to him. Tomorrow he hoped they would be home and safe. And then what? What would happen to him and Harper? Could they try again to regain what they had lost, or had too much time passed and too many things happened for that to ever be possible?

Chapter Sixteen

"Ryker is missing. I'm worried about him." Wanda and Steve Vernon had been waiting for Sheriff Travis Walker when he showed up at the sheriff's department a little after eight o'clock Saturday morning. Adelaide summoned him to the lobby before he had even poured his first cup of coffee. He found Ryker's parents pacing the small reception area. Wanda didn't bother to say hello before voicing her concerns.

"When did you last see him?" Travis asked.

"Night before last." Steve Vernon had his son's dark hair and square chin, though his eyes were a lighter brown and his skin more weathered. "He said good-night and went upstairs, but I saw his light was still on when I went up to bed."

"I thought I heard him leave close to midnight," Wanda said. "I was lying there in bed, unable to sleep, and I heard the stairs creak, then the back door. I thought he was going for a drive to clear his head. I was waiting for him to return, but I must have finally drifted off. When we got up Friday morning, he wasn't there, but he often leaves before we're awake. I was annoyed when I didn't hear from him all day, but when he didn't show up for dinner, or after that, I got really worried. I wanted to call you right then, but Steve persuaded me we should wait."

"I figured he was out searching for Charlotte," Steve said. "I didn't want to embarrass him by contacting his boss."

Travis had spent most of the previous day in a spotter plane, flying over the mining district in search of the white Jeep Mick Davis was supposedly driving, or anything else out of the ordinary. Most of his deputies had been assigned to patrol the network of Jeep roads in the mountains. No one had come up with anything. "I was out all yesterday, searching," he said. "I didn't see any sign of Ryker or his vehicle."

Wanda hugged her arms across her chest. "I can't believe this is happening—first Charlotte, now Ryker." She had striking features, with high cheekbones in a heart-shaped face, her long, dark hair just beginning to show gray at the temples.

Travis had a vague memory that she had once been a local beauty queen. Miss Rayford County or something like that. "I assume you've tried calling and texting him?" he asked.

"Of course. But I'm not getting any answer."

Steve rubbed his wife's shoulder. "If he's in the mountains, he probably doesn't have cell service."

Wanda shrugged off his hand. "Ryker said Mick Davis has a criminal record, but he wouldn't tell me what for. What if he went after Ryker? Either because he's Charlotte's dad or because he's a law enforcement officer?"

"We don't have any reason to believe Mick has anything personally against Ryker," Travis said.

The front door to the sheriff's department opened and Valerie Stanick entered. She stopped and frowned at the Vernons, then focused on the sheriff. "Harper didn't come back to her apartment last night," she said. "She's not answering her phone, and she didn't show up for work yesterday. That's not like her at all."

Wanda clutched her husband's arm. "Maybe Harper is with Ryker."

"What would she be doing with Ryker?" Valerie put a definite chill behind her words. Like Wanda, Valerie had the kind of beauty that didn't fade with age. Her blond hair was swept back off her forehead and her hazel eyes seemed capable of looking right through a man. Travis found himself squaring his shoulders and standing up a little straighter as he faced her.

"Harper has been helping Ryker search for Charlotte," Wanda said. "They spent at least one afternoon driving around the mining district, searching for them. Harper didn't tell you?"

Valerie's lips tightened. She addressed the sheriff. "Where is Ryker now?"

"We don't know." Steve Vernon spoke up. "We came here to report that he didn't come home last night."

"And you think he just ran off with my daughter? Eloped?"

"Of course not!" Wanda's voice rose. "Ryker wouldn't leave town as long as Charlotte is missing. He wouldn't. I'm sure the two of them are somewhere, looking for her." She turned to the sheriff. "But what if Ryker's truck broke down, or they got lost hiking?"

"If Harper is hurt, I blame your son," Valerie said to Steve.

"Ryker hasn't done anything wrong," Wanda protested.

"Ryker would never hurt Harper," Steve said. "He cares about her a great deal. He always has." He looked sadder, and older, as he spoke.

"I'll ask my deputies to keep a lookout for them," Travis

said. "We're sending a drone up in some areas today to do some lower-altitude searches."

"Have you heard anything at all about Charlotte?" Wanda asked.

"When we picked up her mother, she said Charlotte was with Mick Davis," Travis said. "We don't know any more than that at this time."

Wanda couldn't see Valerie's face from where she was standing, but Travis could. Valerie looked as if she was on the verge of sobbing. He put a hand on Wanda's arm. "I promise we'll look for Ryker. And for Harper. I'm sure you're right and the two of them are hunting for Charlotte. I'll keep you posted."

Steve moved in to take his wife's arm and steer her toward the door. "Thank you, Travis," he said, and they left.

Valerie nodded, and hurried after them.

Adelaide moved in and handed Travis a cup of coffee. "I'm concerned that Wanda is right and Ryker and Harper are lost or have had car trouble," she said.

"I'll alert the deputies to be on the lookout for them while they're searching for Charlotte." Travis turned toward his office.

"I hope we find that little girl soon."

"I do, too." He knew all the statistics about missing persons—the longer someone, especially a child, stayed missing, the less chance of finding them. Trails went cold. And anything could happen in the rough country where Charlotte and Mick had last been seen.

HARPER SCOOTED CLOSER to the campfire, trying to warm her icy hands. She had forgotten how cold even summer nights could be at this elevation. The bivy bags had kept them from freezing last night, but they hadn't offered much in the way of comfort. She had awakened every couple of hours, sore and stiff from lying on the hard ground. She had heard Ryker tossing and turning, too. Only Charlotte had slept soundly.

When Ryker had risen shortly before dawn to feed sticks and broken tree limbs into the fire, Harper had joined him and tried not to think about how wonderful a cup of coffee with cream and sugar would be right now. She and Ryker had shared part of the remaining bar, along with an energy gel that was probably past its prime but better than nothing. When Charlotte woke, Harper made her a cup of cocoa from a packet she found at the bottom of her pack. The adults drank water, and Harper washed down a couple of ibuprofen from her first aid kit, though it did little to relieve the headache that pounded at her temples. *We're going to be home in a few hours*, she reminded herself. She was going to shower, eat and take a nap. By tomorrow all of this misery would be only a memory.

Ryker sat on a section of log across from the little blaze and studied a map he had spread out across his knees. "I think we're in here somewhere," he said, and stabbed his index finger at the map.

Harper moved over until she could see the position he indicated among the contour lines of the map. "If we head east, then south, we should reach this drainage here," he said. He indicated another spot on the map. "If we follow that, we should reach the road here." His finger traced a path to the dark line that designated the road. "From there we can walk back up the road about half a mile to the parking area where we left our cars."

It was a lot of walking, over rough terrain, but knowing they had a plan lifted Harper's spirits. "That's terrific." She rested her hand on his shoulder, enjoying the reassuring strength of him. Last night by the fire she had felt so close to him. As if they were starting to mend the rift that had separated them for so long. She told herself not to get her hopes up, but her heart wasn't listening to logic.

"Finished!" Charlotte, wrapped in one of the bivy bags, held their single cup aloft. A faint chocolate moustache adorned her upper lip, along with a few crumbs from one of the protein bars.

"That's great." Harper took the cup and smoothed back the girl's hair, which was a mess of dirty tangles. "How are you feeling this morning?"

"Okay." Charlotte looked to her father. "Are we going home today?"

"We are." He stood, then scooped her into his arms. "We're going to go home and your grandmother is going to make you whatever you want for supper."

"Pizza!" Charlotte didn't hesitate in her choice. "And trees, with butter."

Ryker laughed, then, seeing Harper's puzzled look, said, "Broccoli is Charlotte's favorite vegetable."

"They do look like little trees," Harper said. She smiled at Charlotte, who answered with a grin. Harper's heart flipped over in her chest. Even if she didn't already care for Ryker, she was completely besotted with his little girl.

They packed up camp, made sure the campfire was extinguished, then set out, Ryker regularly checking the map he had downloaded to his phone to make sure they stayed on course. If she had been fed and caffeinated, Harper might have enjoyed the hike more, but she was grateful for the mild weather and the mostly-downhill route they followed. She walked behind Ryker, with Charlotte between them, and passed the time admiring his strong shoulders beneath his pack, narrow hips and attractive backside. She smiled to herself, remembering sitting behind him in high school chemistry and amusing herself this same way.

When Charlotte began to tire, they took turns carrying her. Harper balanced the little girl on one hip. She wasn't a very large child, and seemed so vulnerable with her tangled hair, dirty clothes and scraped knees. A wave of tenderness washed over Harper as she held the child close.

Charlotte studied her, and Harper wondered what she was thinking. The scrutiny was unnerving, so she tried to break the tension with conversation. "What's your favorite color?" she asked.

"Pink. What's yours?"

"Blue."

"Blue is my dad's favorite color, too."

Harper nodded. She had known this, though she hadn't thought about it for a long time. "I guess pizza is your favorite food," she said. "What kind?"

"Cheese," Charlotte said. "Dad likes sausage."

Harper nodded. She remembered that from the pizzas the two of them had shared in school. Back then, Ryker could eat an entire large pizza by himself and never seem full.

But never mind what she already knew about Ryker. Here was her chance to discover things she didn't know. "Does your dad read to you?" she asked. "Bedtime stories?"

"Sometimes. Grandma reads to me most of the time. Dad sometimes sits with me while she reads, when he doesn't have to work."

Harper pictured the three of them—the little girl tucked into bed, Ryker on one side and Wanda on the other. A little family. Would there ever be room for another woman in that scene? Room for her?

"Daddy is a sheriff's deputy," Charlotte said. "He helps people when they're in trouble."

"Yes, he does."

Charlotte studied her a moment longer, her gaze traveling over each detail of Harper's face. Harper remained still, wondering what this little girl thought of her. "What do you do?" Charlotte asked when she had completed her inspection.

"I draw maps," Harper said.

Charlotte's forehead wrinkled. "How do you do that?" she asked.

"Do you remember the map your dad was looking at this morning?" Harper asked. "He was figuring out which way we needed to walk to get back to his truck. Lots of lines on a piece of paper?"

Charlotte nodded, though she still looked doubtful. "That's what I do," Harper said. "I draw maps like that one. Or maps of towns that show where the houses and streets are located. Or pictures of hiking trails. Or ski trails."

Clearly, Charlotte was unimpressed. "Do you have a dog?" she asked.

"No. Do you?"

"No, but I want one. Do you think when I get home Grandma and Grandpa will be so happy to see me, they'll let me get a puppy?"

Harper suppressed a laugh. If it were up to her, she would run straight out to find a puppy for this little darling. "You never know," she said instead.

"I want to get down now," Charlotte said, so Harper set her carefully on the ground and she ran ahead to catch up with Ryker.

They hiked for three hours, scarcely stopping to switch off carrying Charlotte, or to drink the last of their water. Harper's head and shoulders and back and legs ached, but she kept putting one foot in front of the other, focused on getting to the truck. She could sit down there. Lock the doors. They would be safe. The memory of Mick brandishing the axe, then firing a gun at them had disturbed her dreams, and all morning she had found herself searching their surroundings for any sign of him.

The drainage had been formed from snowmelt trickling down during the spring thaw. It was dry now, littered with loose boulders and the stubby new growth of saplings and shrubs. They had to pick their way as the elevation dropped, avoiding loose rocks and unstable soil. The sun beat down and a fly repeatedly buzzed in Harper's ear. She swatted it away and focused on their destination. A little before noon they emerged onto the road. She had been taking another turn carrying Charlotte, and Ryker took the child from her. "Not much farther to go now," he said.

When they drew in sight of the parking area a short time later, her heart beat faster as she recognized her Subaru, looking dusty and a little forlorn by itself on the side of the road. "Where is your truck?" she asked Ryker.

"I don't know." He picked up his speed, trotting the final hundred yards, then stopped in the spot beside her car where his truck had been parked.

Harper looked all around them, but there was no sign of the truck. "We disabled Mick's Jeep so he couldn't get away in it," Ryker said. "He must have hiked here and stolen my truck."

"We still have my car." Harper pulled the keys from the side pocket of her pack and pressed the button on the fob to unlock the doors. All she wanted was to get the three of them back to the safety of town.

Ryker set Charlotte on the ground and slipped off his pack. "As soon as we have a cell signal I'll call the sheriff and let him know Mick probably has my truck."

Harper slid into the driver's seat and inserted the key into the ignition. Then she merely sat for a moment, enjoying the feeling of sitting down on a soft surface. Ryker settled Charlotte in the back seat and fastened the seat belt over her hips. "We don't have a booster seat for you," he said. "But we'll have to make do for now. You have to promise to sit back and be still."

"I promise."

Harper turned the key in the ignition. *Tick, tick, tick*...

She stared at Ryker, wide eyed. "Pop the hood," he said.

She reached under the dash and pulled the handle to release the latch. He got out and raised the hood and peered into the engine compartment. He swore.

"Daddy said a bad word," Charlotte said.

Harper got out and joined Ryker at the front of the car. "What's wrong?" she asked.

"He ripped out every wire he could reach," he said. "Someone did. But I'm sure it was Mick. And he flattened three of the tires."

She hadn't even noticed the tires in her eagerness to sit inside the car. She might have said a few bad words herself, but she didn't have the energy. "What do we do now?" she asked.

He lowered the hood. "We're going to have to walk. At least until we get a cell signal and can call for help."

She could have lain down then and there and wept, but that wouldn't help anything. Ryker must have read her thoughts from her expression. "I'd offer to go for help by myself," he said. "But I don't like the idea of leaving you and Charlotte alone, in case Mick comes back."

"No. We stay together." She went back to the driver's seat and leaned in. "Charlotte, honey, my car is broken," she said. "We're going to have to walk until we can call for help."

Charlotte began to cry, and Harper felt tears well in her own eyes. "I know, honey. I feel that way, too," she said. "But we're just going to have to do it. No pizza until we do."

Charlotte sobbed harder. Ryker leaned in, unbuckled her, and pulled her close. She continued to sob as he led the way down the road. Harper locked the car, with their packs inside, and followed. One foot in front of the other. And hoped Mick Davis didn't decide to come back.

Chapter Seventeen

Jamie stifled a yawn, and shifted in the driver's seat of her sheriff's department SUV. Her daughter had been fussier than usual last night, with Jamie and her husband, Nate, taking turns getting up with her. It had taken a very hot shower and a lot of hot coffee to get going this morning, but the thought of Ryker's little girl out there somewhere with a man who wasn't her father had spurred her on. Today, she decided to focus on some of the more remote roads in the mining district. Dwight had said he had driven up there the day before yesterday and discovered the road to the mine blocked by a rockslide, making it unlikely that Mick Davis and Charlotte were up there. But Jamie had felt compelled to check it out for herself. Maybe Davis had cleared a path around the rockslide, or there was another route they hadn't explored yet.

She was making her way up the county road toward the Jeep route when a black Ford pickup passed her on the left. Jamie stared hard at the vehicle. That looked like Ryker's truck. She pressed down harder on the gas, trying to catch up. She came around a curve in time to see the truck turn onto the same Jeep road she had been headed for. She made the turn also, and tried to get close enough to read the license plate number. Dust boiled up beneath the truck's tires, obscuring the plate.

The sheriff had sent a call out earlier that Ryker and Harper Stanick were both missing. "We think they were searching for Charlotte, but they may have run into car trouble so be on the lookout," the sheriff said.

Jamie sped up, gritting her teeth as the SUV bounced up the washboarded road. She could see the truck more clearly now, though she still couldn't read the license plate. The back window was streaked with dirt, but she could make out a single occupant, wearing a dark windbreaker, much like the black Rayford County Sheriff's Department jacket Jamie herself wore. And the driver's hair was covered by a black knit cap. Hadn't she seen Ryker in a similar cap recently?

She tried to get closer, but the truck pulled away, kicking up gravel that hit her windshield. She let off the accelerator and flashed her lights, but the truck didn't stop, so she hit the siren. One loud whoop. The truck sped up even more.

As if he was trying to get away from her.

She pulled to the side of the road and shifted into Park, then keyed her radio. Signal repeaters positioned around the county were supposed to enable communication from anywhere, but depending on the terrain and the weather, they weren't always reliable. "Dispatch, this is Rayford County Sheriff's Department Unit 16."

"Hello, Jamie. What can I do for you?" Dispatcher Sally Graham's friendly voice responded.

"I'm headed south on the road up to the Jack's Peak trailhead. I'm following a truck that looks like the one Ryker drives. And there's a man in the cab who could be Ryker, but he's not stopping, even though I let him know I'm behind him."

"Hang on, I'm going to connect you with the sheriff."

As she waited, Jamie stared at the cloud of dust ahead that marked the truck's progress. Ryker or whoever was driving the vehicle was well above the posted speed limit of twenty-five miles per hour for these Jeep roads. In some places, even twenty-five was too much speed for the narrow, rutted tracks and sharp curves.

"Jamie, you think you've spotted Ryker?" Travis's clipped voice came on the line.

"Yes, sir. He passed me on the county road and turned onto the Jeep road up toward the Jack's Peak trail."

"You're sure it's Ryker?"

"No, sir. It looks like his truck, but I can't get close enough to read the license plate, and I can only tell you there's a person driving who appears to be a man about Ryker's height and build. But he was clearly trying to get away from me. He wouldn't stop even when I flashed my lights and hit the siren."

"Any passengers in the vehicle?"

"Not that I could see."

"Can you still see the vehicle?" Travis asked.

"Just the dust cloud he made. But I don't know of anywhere around here to turn off the road."

"Proceed cautiously," Travis said. "I'll send backup out your way."

"Have you heard anything from Ryker or Harper?"

"Not yet. Whoever this is, keep your distance until backup arrives."

"Yes, sir." She ended the transmission and steered her SUV back into the road. Ryker had no reason to run away from her, so maybe whoever was driving that car wasn't him. But if that was true, what had happened to Ryker?

RYKER SHIFTED CHARLOTTE from one hip to the other and trudged across the uneven terrain, keeping parallel to the road as much as possible, but out of sight of any driver— particularly Mick Davis—who might pass. Every joint in his body ached, and his head pounded. He was furious at Mick and Kim, and at himself, too. If he had taken the trouble to investigate Mick more thoroughly when Kim first got together with him, maybe he could have been better prepared for the possibility that the two of them might try something like this. At the very least he could have prepared Charlotte to resist an attempt by Kim to take her without permission. He had wanted to believe the best of his ex, but that attitude had put their daughter in danger.

He glanced over his shoulder at Harper, who walked with her head down, back bent. She looked weary and defeated, and guilt stabbed at him. He had put her in danger, too. As if he hadn't put her through enough in their time together, what with the surprise pregnancy, her parents' disapproval, her banishment to Florida, and his inability to be with her when she needed him most. He had been thrilled to find she didn't harbor resentment for all of that, but now he had pulled her into this mess. He wouldn't blame her if she didn't want anything to do with him after this.

She lifted her head and smiled. "Do you need me to take Charlotte for a bit?" she asked, and hurried to catch up with him.

"Do you want Harper to carry you for a little bit?" he asked Charlotte.

"No." Charlotte pressed her forehead into his shoulder.

"Maybe you'd like to get down and walk on your own for a little bit?" Ryker asked.

"No!"

Harper's eyes met his, her expression sympathetic. "She's probably worn out," she said.

They were all worn out. Ryker dug his phone from his pocket and checked to see if he had a signal yet. Nope. And his battery was getting low. He had turned it off overnight to conserve the battery but now that it kept searching for a tower, it was draining fast.

Harper stopped and put a hand on Ryker's arm, stopping him. "I think I hear a car coming," she said.

He raised his head. Yes, that was the distant crunch of tires on gravel, and the whine of an engine straining up a grade. "Maybe we can catch a ride," he said.

"Unless it's Mick," she said.

He nodded. "Let's get out of sight and take a look. If it isn't Mick, we can probably run after it and get the driver's attention."

They moved farther off the road into a clump of sagebrush, and crouched down. Moments later, Ryker's own truck rocketed past, rocks pinging as they hit the undercarriage, suspension protesting as the vehicle charged in and out of ruts. "He's going to tear up my truck, driving like that on these roads," he said.

"Was Mick driving?" Harper asked.

"I didn't see who it was," Ryker said. "But it had to be Mick. He's probably heading back to the parking area to see if he can intercept us."

"He'll see our packs in my car and know we've been there," Harper said. "What do we do?"

"We keep walking, but we have to stay off the road and out of sight."

They stood and set out again, but Charlotte balked. "I don't want to walk anymore!" she wailed. "I'm tired and hot and hungry. I want to stop. I want to go home." She sobbed, tears dampening the front of Ryker's shirt.

He rubbed her back, frustrated by his inability to do anything to help her. "I know you're hungry and hot and tired," he said. "Harper and I are too. I promise, we're doing everything we can to get you home. But to do that, we have to keep moving."

"Let me take her for a while," Harper said. "That way you'll have both hands free."

She didn't say she wanted him to be able to draw his weapon if Mick returned, but he was sure she was thinking it. He certainly was. If Mick did return and find them, it would be up to Ryker to protect both Charlotte and Harper. He wasn't going to let anything happen to them.

Charlotte screamed as Harper peeled her away from Ryker, but Harper merely cuddled her close. She whispered in Charlotte's ear and before long the child calmed and clung to Harper. "I think we're ready now," Harper said.

Ryker turned to lead the way back toward the county road when he heard his truck returning, the roar of the engine rapidly growing louder. Once again, they dove for shelter, this time in a trio of piñons clustered close to the road.

The truck wasn't moving as fast this time. Ryker could clearly see Mick as he passed by them, the driver's window rolled down. A short distance past them, he stopped the vehicle in the middle of the road. "What's he doing?" Harper whispered.

Ryker shook his head. He reached back and eased his pistol out of its holster and brought it forward. The truck door opened and Mick slid out. He stood for a moment, looking around, then turned and began walking toward them. Sun glinted off the pistol in his hand.

He stopped when he was only a few feet from them and

aimed the gun at the clump of trees where they waited. "Get out of there and stand up slowly," he said. "Don't try anything."

Harper stared at Ryker, wide-eyed. Charlotte whimpered and reached for him. Ryker shook his head. He still wasn't sure Mick knew they were here. Maybe he was only guessing.

"Do it!" Mick shouted, and fired the gun. Bark tore from one of the tree trunks as the bullet hit it. Charlotte screamed so loudly Ryker worried she had been hit. "She's okay," Harper said. She smoothed the girl's hair. "She's okay."

"Stay down," Ryker said. He laid his pistol on the ground, right beside Harper, then slowly stood, his hands in the air.

"The woman and the girl, too," Mick said. "Now!"

Harper popped up, Charlotte beside her. Harper gripped Charlotte's hand.

"Throw out your gun," Mick ordered. "I know you've got one."

Ryker looked down at the pistol. "It's on the ground," he said. "I have to bend down to pick it up."

"Leave it, then, and step out here."

They did as he ordered, Ryker first, then Harper and Charlotte.

"Why didn't you leave when you could?" Harper asked. "You had the truck. You could be in New Mexico by now."

"I came back for Charlotte," he said. He wore a battered black baseball cap that shielded his eyes from view, but his words alone were enough to send a shiver down Ryker's spine.

"What do you want with her?" he asked.

"I like her. And I think she'd be useful. If I've got her with me as a hostage, the cops will have to let me go to save her. No one wants to see a little girl get hurt."

"You'll never lay a hand on her," Ryker said.

"You talk tough, but I'm the one with the gun. Come out here before I decide to shoot you. Or maybe I'll shoot your girlfriend. How would you like that?"

Harper glanced at Ryker. Then he realized she wasn't looking at him but past him, down the road. Then he heard what had caught her attention. The crunch of tires on gravel.

"Hurry up!" Mick shouted.

Ryker took a step toward the truck. Harper started after him, then stopped. He looked back to see her crouched on the ground, next to Charlotte. She stared into Charlotte's face. "You need to run," she told the little girl. "As fast and as far away from Mick as you can. Your dad and I will distract him, then we'll catch up with you later."

Charlotte looked up at Ryker. He nodded. "Run," he said, keeping his voice soft, but trying to convey the urgency of the matter.

Harper stood and Charlotte ran. Ryker bounded down the slope to the road, hoping his movements would distract Mick. "Hey!" Mick shouted, and raised the pistol as if to fire. But the wail of a siren shattered the stillness, and he swiveled toward the sound. Two Rayford County Sheriff's Department SUVs hurtled toward them.

The first SUV slid sideways and stopped, blocking the road. Mick turned toward it, mouth open. He was still holding the gun, but he held it at his side, the muzzle pointed at the dirt. Ryker stared at the weapon for half a second before making his decision. He rushed forward and threw Mick to the ground.

The gun went off, the bullet striking the ground. Then Deputy Jamie Douglas was out of the SUV and she and Ryker subdued Mick. They had him handcuffed, face down in the road, when Travis and Gage Walker joined them.

Ryker nodded at the sheriff and his brother, then turned to look toward the roadside. "Charlotte!" he shouted.

"It's okay. We're both right here." Harper walked down the road toward them, Charlotte in her arms.

Ryker met them and took Charlotte, then put his free hand on her shoulder. "Are you okay?" he asked.

She nodded. "I am now. What about you?"

He fit Charlotte more securely on his hip, then took Harper's hand in his. Behind him, he could hear Jamie reciting the Miranda warning to Mick as she and Gage transferred him to Gage's SUV. "I'm okay now," he said. As okay as he'd ever be again.

RYKER WAS STILL holding Harper's hand when the sheriff walked up to them. "Your parents and Harper's mother were at the sheriff's department first thing this morning to report the two of you missing," he said. "Have you been with Mick Davis all this time?"

"We tracked him down to the Lucky Six Mine, where he'd set up camp," Ryker said. "We took Charlotte and got away on foot. We got off track and had to work our way back to the road. Mick was looking for us and spotted us. You all showed up just in time."

"Your truck passed me on the county road and turned off onto this Jeep trail." Jamie moved up beside the sheriff. "We had been alerted to look for you, but when you didn't pull over when I signaled you, I got worried enough to call for help."

"Come on," Travis said. "You can give your statements back at the office. Your parents are waiting for you."

They rode to town in the sheriff's SUV, Ryker in the front passenger seat, Harper in the back next to Charlotte in a car seat Travis unearthed from the back of the vehicle.

"My twins aren't big enough for this yet, but we keep a few spares at the department to hand out to people who might need them," he explained as he buckled it into the vehicle.

Harper studied the back of Ryker's head as they drove. Charlotte fell asleep and Harper felt if she closed her eyes and allowed herself, she might doze off, too. "You said my mother reported me missing?" she asked Travis.

"Yes. She walked in a few minutes after Ryker's parents came to ask us to look for him." He glanced in the rear-view mirror, catching her eye. "When Ryker's mother said she thought you and Ryker might be together, your mother asked if the two of you had eloped."

"Eloped?" Ryker sounded horrified at the idea—because her mother had asked, or because he was appalled at the idea? Not that Harper wanted to run away this minute to get married, but his reaction made her queasy. Was the idea of the two of them married really so awful?

At the station, they had scarcely entered the front doors before Wanda and Steve Vernon surrounded them. "Charlotte, I'm so happy to see you." Tears streamed down Wanda's face as she gathered the little girl close.

Steve embraced his son. "I knew you'd find her," he said.

Harper took a step back, not wanting to intrude on this family reunion. She spotted her mother and father on the other side of the room and went to join them. Her father hugged her. "I'm glad you're okay, sweetheart," he said.

Valerie studied her daughter. "You look like you had a rough night," she said. She stared at Harper's hair, which probably needed combing.

"Did you really think Ryker and I eloped?" It wasn't the way she had planned to start the conversation with her mother—the words burst out on their own accord.

The line between Valerie's eyebrows deepened. "You've never behaved rationally around that man," she said.

"Ryker isn't *that man*," Harper said. "He's someone I care about. Very much."

Valerie started to speak, but Harper interrupted. "I'm an adult now," she said. "You can't send me off to Florida because you don't like the decision I made."

"Yes, you are." Her dad put his arm around her. "Your mom and I will be here for you, no matter what happens."

Valerie pressed her lips together. Harper couldn't tell if it was because she was trying not to say something she might later regret—or because she was trying not to cry. Valerie looked down at the floor, then up again, and said. "I wasn't trying to ruin your life when I sent you to Florida. I was trying to keep you from making a big mistake. You were too young, and I didn't think Ryker was the right man for you."

"Because you thought he had something to do with his cousin's death."

She flushed. "I wasn't the only one who believed that. And they never found anyone else who was responsible, did they?"

"Ryker didn't have anything to do with Aiden's abduction," Harper said. "The DNA evidence proved that, but I knew he wasn't capable of such a thing."

"I didn't know that," Valerie said. "And I had to protect you. When you have a child of your own one day, you'll understand."

Harper thought of how much she had wanted to protect Charlotte, and she hugged her mother. "It's okay, Mom. I don't think it hurt anything that Ryker and I both had time to grow up. And I'm sorry I worried you two."

"You're safe now," her dad said. "That's all that mat-

ters." He joined in the hug and Harper savored this feeling
of closeness. As often as they had clashed, she could see
now her mother's actions had come from a place of love.
Time had given her a new perspective.

She hoped the years had given her courage, too. Courage to stand up to her parents, sure. But also courage to go
after the man she wanted. Or at least to find out how he
really felt about her, knowing she might not get the answer
she wanted to hear.

THREE HOURS LATER, Ryker stood at the door to Charlotte's
bedroom, watching her sleep. She lay curled on her side
beneath her pink comforter, a daisy-shaped night-light giving off a soft glow. She smelled of strawberry bath gel, her
clean blond hair spread out on her pillow. She had eaten
pizza and ice cream, and had made it halfway through a
bedtime story before she had fallen asleep. Ryker, having
showered and shaved and eaten, should have been headed
for his own bed. But energy buzzed through him, and his
brain kept replaying scenes from the past few days, from
the shoot-out with Mick Davis to last night's campfire conversation with Harper.

His mother moved in beside him. "I can't stop checking to make sure she really is still here," Wanda said softly.

"I know." He let out a long breath. "But she is here. And
Kim and Mick are in jail. She's safe. We all are." Logically,
he believed this to be true. It would probably take a little
longer for his emotions to settle down and accept that, but
he trusted it would come.

"What about Harper?"

He met his mother's gaze. Her expression was one he
had seen so many times in his life, one that said she had
an opinion on the situation under discussion, but wanted to

hear his take before she gave advice. Whether he wanted her opinion or not, he was going to get it and no sense arguing. As she had said more than once when he was growing up, "I'm your mother and I have an obligation to try to teach you at least a little of what I know."

"Harper…is complicated," he said. "My job takes so much of my time, and Charlotte deserves the rest."

"Lots of people manage to juggle jobs and children and relationships."

"I know, but—"

Wanda laid a hand on his arm. "Do you love her?"

He hesitated only a few seconds before he nodded. "Yes."

"Then you should tell her."

He looked back at his sleeping daughter, a dozen reasons why that would not be a good idea filling his head.

"I think Charlotte would like to have a mother," Wanda said. "And I think you shouldn't be alone."

"If it doesn't work out between us, it will hurt Charlotte, too." And it would hurt him. That possibility frightened him more than he would ever admit.

"I remember the way the two of you were together, even when you were seventeen and eighteen. And I've seen the two of you together now. Don't let fear of something that probably won't ever happen keep you from being happy now."

He turned back to his mother. She smiled up at him. "Go on. Charlotte isn't going to wake up for hours, and you won't rest until you've seen Harper."

He kissed her cheek. "How did you get to be so smart?"

"I raised a smart boy. I had to keep up with you."

"Can I borrow the Jeep?" Ryker asked. "The evidence team is still going over my truck."

"Of course, dear. Tell Harper we said hello."

He retrieved the keys and walked out to the Jeep, parked at the side of the house. Movement in the bushes brought him up short and he pivoted toward the sound, just as Gary Langley emerged. The light from a window flashed on something bright as the older man lunged, and Ryker instinctively dodged out of the way, then felt the sharp edge of a knife slicing his arm.

Langley lunged again, but Ryker shoved back, then kicked one leg out to trip the old man. Langley fell hard, taking Ryker down with him. The two men rolled, the knife cutting Ryker again. He felt the sting, and the sticky warmth of blood, but adrenaline numbed the pain. He smashed his fist against Langley's jaw, then grabbed his wrist and bent it back. The knife rattled against the gravel of the driveway. Ryker knelt on the older man's chest and pinned both arms at his sides. "Try anything else and I swear I'll break your arm," Ryker said.

Langley blinked up at him, transformed once more from angry predator to weak old man. "I thought I could take you by surprise and silence you before anyone heard," he said.

"Why would you try to kill me?" Ryker asked.

"You were asking too many questions about things that happened a long time ago."

"You kidnapped Aiden and killed him."

Langley turned his head to the side. "I'm not saying anything."

Ryker rolled Langley onto his stomach, and used his own bootlaces to tie his hands. Then he stood and pulled out his phone to call the sheriff. "Gary Langley attacked me with a knife outside my home," he said.

The sheriff arrived a few minutes later, along with an ambulance. Steve and Wanda emerged from the house and Wanda turned pale at the sight of the blood running down

Ryker's arms. "It's okay, Mom," he said. "It's going to be okay."

Two deputies put Langley in restraints and the sheriff interviewed Ryker while Hannah cleaned and bandaged the cuts on his arms, none of which were very deep. "Your jacket protected you," she said as she applied rows of Steri-Strips across the longest wound. "But you'll need to be careful of infection, and make sure you're up to date on your tetanus vaccine."

She left them and Travis said, "I did some checking and Langley was asked to resign from his coaching position because there had been complaints he was paying the wrong kind of attention to some of the kids."

"Aiden played soccer for a little while," Ryker said. He buttoned up the new shirt he had asked his mom to bring from the house. "He probably knew Langley."

"I'm going to do some more digging. Aiden might not be the only child he harmed."

"That accident he had likely saved a lot of kids," Ryker said. "He probably thought he had gotten away with Aiden's murder, and then I came back and started asking questions."

"Questions that should have been asked years ago," Travis said. "We're going to check his DNA. If it's a match to that found on Aiden's body, he won't have a chance to hurt anyone else."

Ryker nodded. He had no doubt the DNA would be a match. He stood. "Is that all you need from me?"

Travis nodded. "Get some rest. We'll finish up the paperwork in the morning."

But Ryker had no intention of resting. He drove to Harper's apartment, grateful she had her own place. He thought he could deal with her parents when the time came, but he didn't really want them witnessing this particular conversation.

Harper answered the door wearing a clean T-shirt and shorts, barefoot with her toenails painted pink. Her hair was damp and her cheeks flushed, and the air around her smelled of vanilla. Her gaze shifted to the single bandage on the side of his face. "Ryker! Is everything okay?"

"Can I come in?"

"Sure." She held the door wider and he moved past her into a living room furnished with a sofa and chair, and what looked like an antique rocking chair. There were shelves of books and plants, and lots of pictures on the walls, from local landscapes to photographs of people he didn't know. "What happened?" she asked, and gestured to the bandage.

"Gary Langley attacked me outside my house tonight."

"Who is Gary Langley?"

"I think he's the person who kidnapped and killed Aiden. I've been looking into the case. He was a youth soccer coach and local handyman when Aiden was abducted. A neighbor reported seeing a truck that looked like Langley's the night Aiden disappeared, but it was never properly followed up on. Langley found out I was taking a closer look at him and decided to try to stop me."

"Ryker! You could have been killed."

"But I wasn't. And Langley is behind bars and will probably stay there for a long time. Maybe the rest of his life." That knowledge energized him, even though he ought to be exhausted. He looked around the room again, and focused on a large map that hung over the mantel of a gas fireplace. He moved closer and realized it was a map of Eagle Mountain, hand-drawn with all the local landmarks and businesses carefully labeled.

"Did you draw this?" he asked.

She came to stand beside him, close enough he realized the vanilla aroma was coming from her hair. "I did. You can get a copy of your own, on a smaller scale, from the visitor's bureau." She hugged her arms across her chest. "It was one of the first projects I did when I moved back. It helped me get to know my hometown again."

"I'm glad you came back," he said.

"Are you?"

Was that hurt he heard in her voice, or merely his own doubts coloring his interpretation? He turned to her. "I love you," he said. "I'm not sure I ever stopped but seeing you again, I knew. I just didn't know if that was enough to make up for all the mistakes I made before."

She dropped her hands to her sides, her expression puzzled. "What mistakes did you make? I'm the one who left town without even telling you where I was going."

"Because your parents wouldn't let you. I knew that. But I should have tried harder to find you. I left you pregnant and alone with strangers."

"I was with my aunt. And she was kind, even if she wasn't exactly thrilled to have me with her."

"But you had to go through losing the baby without me there."

"I did." She moved closer, and slid her arms around his waist. "But I never blamed you. I blamed my parents—especially my mom. But I never blamed you."

"Why not?"

She smiled. "I guess because I still loved you so much. In my eyes, you could do no wrong."

"If you had only known I was off getting involved with a woman I never should have gone out with, much less married. A woman who would leave me for an ex-con and return years later to kidnap our daughter and lead me to dragging you along to chase after her boyfriend, who could have ended up killing you." A tremor shook him at the last words, and Harper hugged him more tightly.

"What happened in the past isn't as important as what we do now," she said. "I love you and I love Charlotte, too. I want to be a part of your lives."

He looked into her eyes, and all the fear left him. He wanted to be with her. He wanted Charlotte to know her better. He wanted the three of them to make the family they had been denied before. All that hope didn't leave any room for worry and doubt. "I love you," he said, and kissed her.

In the fairy tales he sometimes read Charlotte, kisses were magical things, turning frogs into princes and waking sleeping beauties. Harper's kiss was like that, breaking the lock he had kept on his emotions. He didn't have to be anywhere or answer to anyone or worry that at any moment she might turn on him. All he had to do was be here with her and enjoy the feel of her body pressed to his, the softness of her lips and the heat that spread through him as she stroked her hands down his back.

She broke the kiss and smiled up at him. "Do you remember the afternoon we sneaked into your house when your parents were away, and made love in your bedroom?" she asked.

"Yes. I wanted you so much, yet I was nervous we would get caught." That afternoon had been both wonderful and awful, since he had felt cheated of the ability to fully enjoy it.

"No parents to interrupt us here," she said, a wicked gleam in her eye.

He took her hand and kissed her palm. "Where's the bedroom?" he asked.

Later, he couldn't have told anyone what the room looked like, except that the mattress was soft and the sheets cool and silky, and she was beautiful. She was different, yet the same, more mature, more confident, yet the same woman he had loved all along. Making love to her was new and exciting and so familiar. He remembered what she liked and how she made him feel. He wanted to touch and kiss every inch of her, yet his body—and her urgent movements and breathy sighs—told him neither of them wanted to wait the time that might take. He settled for kissing his way down her torso, then pausing to gaze up at her. "Do you have a condom?"

She laughed.

"What's so funny?"

She rolled over and opened the drawer of her bedside table and pulled out a strip of foil packets. "I was just thinking that as much as this all feels the same for us, we have at least learned to be a little more responsible." She tore off a packet and thrust it at him. "Just so you know, I bought these after that first day I ran into you, up on Dixon Pass at that accident call."

"Really? The first day?"

"I had hopes."

"Then let's see if we can make a few dreams come true. For both of us." He tore open the packet.

She lay back against the pillows, watching him with an expression that was more erotic than any touch. He rolled on the condom, then moved up to lie beside her. She trailed her fingers down his chest. "One day I'll draw a map of you," she said. "I'll annotate it with all my favorite parts."

"Such as?"

"Here." She kissed his shoulder. "And here." More kisses traced the muscles of his chest. "And definitely down here." She moved lower.

When he could restrain himself no longer, her urged her

up beside him once more. "Work on your map later," he said. "I don't want to wait any longer."

"No. We've waited long enough."

They came together without awkwardness, two people who knew what they needed and were as eager to give as they were to take. They didn't rush, but they didn't waste time, either. When she climaxed she made the same small, joyous sounds she had so long ago, and he couldn't help but smile. Then she reached down and touched him and his own release surged through him and he shouted her name. Which he had never done before, but this time, it felt right. The two of them together felt right, in a way that nothing had in a very long time.

Epilogue

"I promise to love and support you, to stand by your side, and to face together all the ups and downs that life may bring."

"And I promise to love and support *you*, to stand by your side, and to face together all the ups and downs that life may bring."

"By the power invested in me by the state of Colorado, I now pronounce you husband and wife."

Cheers erupted and a trumpet fanfare heralded the bride and groom's exit down the aisle. Harper and Ryker rose to stand with the rest of the guests as Hannah and Jake paraded past their family and friends. Ryker slipped his arm around her. "Were you taking mental notes for our wedding?" he asked.

Harper looked down at the diamond solitaire on the third finger of her left hand. She had only had it a few days, and she couldn't stop admiring it. "Maybe a few." She grinned up at him. "Charlotte has been giving me ideas, though."

"Charlotte has ideas for our wedding?"

"I told her I wanted her to be a bridesmaid, so she asked if she could wear a fancy pink dress. And she thinks I should wear flowers in my hair, like a picture in one of her favorite storybooks. And we should serve pizza at the reception, because everyone likes pizza."

"I like pizza," he said. Then he burst out laughing when he saw her expression. "Okay, no pizza at the reception, but how do you feel about pink dresses and flowers in your hair?"

"The idea is beginning to grow on me. What do you think?"

"I don't care what we do, as long as you and Charlotte are both there. You two are all I need."

"I think it was worth waiting to marry you to hear lines like that one." She kissed his cheek. "You were never this smooth in high school."

"I like to think I've learned a few things over the years." He slid his hand down her hip.

She caught his wrist and directed his hand to her waist. "Let's make our way to the reception."

"Are you in a hurry?" He followed her out of the chapel. The reception was being held at the Alpiner Inn, a short walk down the street.

"I was just thinking," she said. "Your mom isn't expecting you home until late, right?"

"My mom isn't expecting me home at all." He grinned. "Another nice thing about not being a teenager. I don't have to pretend I'm not spending the night with my fiancée."

"In that case, let's leave the reception as soon as we politely can."

"Something urgent you need to do?" he teased.

"Yes. I have a map I need to work on."

"Must be a special map."

"Oh, it is." She laced her fingers with his. "It's going to take me a lifetime to draw, so I need to devote myself to it."

"We should put that in our wedding vows," he said, and pulled her to him.

The guests who exited behind them had to veer around them while he kissed her, but Harper didn't mind. Not that many people in life got a second chance, and she and Ryker weren't going to waste this one.

* * * * *

Look for more books in Cindi Myers's miniseries Eagle Mountain: Criminal History, coming soon!

And if you missed the first book in the series,
Mile High Mystery
is available now, wherever Harlequin Intrigue books are sold!